K. J. PARKER

This special signed edition
is limited to 1000 numbered copies.

This is copy _779_.

DOWNFALL OF THE GODS

DOWNFALL OF THE GODS

K. J. PARKER

Subterranean Press 2016

First Edition

ISBN
978-1-59606-755-4

Subterranean Press
PO Box 190106
Burton, MI 48519

subterraneanpress.com

It's no good," I said. "She won't hear you."

He didn't look round. "Be quiet," he said.

I rather like the acoustics in the Temple. You can hear the slightest sound, clear as a bell, but no annoying echo. I watched him take a moment to compose his mind and return it to sublime thoughts after my boorish interruption. He bowed his head, and his lips started to move. He was mumbling his way through the Greater Confession.

"You have to mean it," I said.

This time he turned round and scowled at me. "What would you know about anything?" he snapped. "Stupid bloody woman."

I pointed out that the Goddess was a woman too. "Get out," he said.

I put his foul temper and terrible manners down to a guilty conscience. There's something about the Temple. Kings, princes, great lords temporal and spiritual seem to feel it more than most—a sort of horribly insistent sense of perspective; the bigger you are, the more it gets to you. I've seen them shed actual tears of remorse, clench their hands in prayer till the fingers go red and the knuckles go white. Curious; it's an imposing building but the actual statue is pretty insipid work, with a definite smirk on her face. Also, the head's slightly too big for the body.

"I forgive you for snapping at me," I said.

"Piss off."

I shrugged. "You wanted me to come here."

He scowled at me. "Wait outside."

"Are you going to be much longer? I'm hungry."

"Out."

I bobbed a curtsey to the statue and retreated up the nave, leaving him with his head bowed, muttering the formulae. He was sincerely unhappy about something, and honestly believed the Goddess was going to make it all right. Touching, in a way. Men genuinely at prayer look just like little boys.

I waited for him in the chancel, occupying my mind by looking at the mosaics on the ceiling. Silly, really; I'd been in the Temple more times than I could remember, and never properly seen them before. Very fine work, I had to admit, though what they had to do with religion escaped me entirely. A middle-aged woman in an expensive dress walked past me, stopped; she noticed the little gold charms dangling from my necklace, the pendant earring in one ear only; conventional badges of the profession, intended to be seen. She gave me that look. "You ought to be ashamed of yourself," she said.

"I am," I replied pleasantly. "Dreadfully."

I don't think she believed me. She swept past, knelt down on a nice soft hassock and started mumbling her imaginary sins. I forgave her.

When you've admired the mosaics and the frescoes and the richly-bejewelled rood screen, there's not an awful lot to do in the Temple. I suppose I should've brought a book, only clients don't like it. What do you want a book for, they ask, were you expecting to be bored? I listened to a few prayers, but there was nothing to get excited about. I'm sorry to say, I get bored easily.

Eventually he finished his confession. He got up slowly, joints cramped from all that kneeling, made his obeisances and hobbled up the nave. "You've been wasting your time," I told him. "And mine, which you've paid for, but that's your business. She won't hear you."

I'd made him genuinely angry. "You don't know anything," he said. "You're just stupid."

Oh dear. "Tell you what," I said, and I took my purse from my sleeve and opened it. "Here's your five gulden back, and here's five more for luck. So nice to have met you. Goodbye."

I held the coins out; he made no effort to take them. "What's got into you today?" he said.

"Me? Nothing. I was just being helpful. I don't like to see someone wasting his breath."

People were staring at us. I'm used to being stared at, naturally, but it made him uncomfortable. "Stop being stupid and put it away," he said. "Come on. We'll be late for the Archdeacon."

"I don't want any lunch," I said. "And I don't want to meet the Archdeacon, he's a nasty old man and his breath smells. Do you want your money or not?"

He grabbed me by the arm and marched me toward the East door. "What's the matter with you?" he said. "Have you gone mad or something?"

I dug my heels in and stopped. He yanked on my arm. He thought he was stronger than me, and could drag me along by main force. I stayed where I was. He stared at me. "What the hell do you think you're doing?" he said.

"I'm going to stay here," I told him. "You go on without me."

"You'll do as you're told."

I shook my head, just a little. I really didn't want a quarrel. He tried to drag me again; this time he really put his back into it. All his life, he'd been used to being strong, proud of his muscles; the wealth and the power he'd been born with, but his strength was genuinely his own, and nobody had given it to him. I stayed where I was. He let go and took a step back.

Bother, I thought; cat's out of the bag. "I'm sorry," I said.

He opened his mouth to speak, but I didn't want to hear it. For as long as it was safe to do so—the downstroke of one heartbeat—I let him see me. Then I shut it off like a tap.

He looked so comical. They always do. Quite often at that point they fall at my feet and grovel, which I don't care for at all. To his credit, he did nothing of the kind; just stared at me. I guess he'd suddenly realised just how much trouble he was in, and that nothing he could do was going to fix it, and the only person who could save him had just refused to do so. No grovelling; just acceptance and despair. I'll say this for him, he had a sort of dignity. Very much a mortal quality, and one I admire and envy.

"She won't hear you," I said. "I'm sorry."

I TOOK A moment to look at it from his point of view.

He's done a really awful thing, a murder, which he sincerely regrets. The consequences of his act don't bear thinking about. He goes to the Temple—fitting it in on his way to a lunch engagement, yes, and taking his prostitute *du jour* with him, but he does go, he makes the effort; and when he's on his knees, as truly abased and humble as he's capable of being, his prayer for forgiveness is unquestionably sincere. He prays. He uses the proper form of words. He means it (I did him an injustice earlier). He is truly sorry. That, surely, ought to be enough. It ought to do the trick.

Then the Goddess, the Lady of the Moon herself, the Queen of Laughter, grants him an epiphany. Saints pray all their lives for one and rarely if ever are they favoured, but he gets a whole half second, the maximum safe dose. The Goddess stands before him in her true form and says, I'm sorry. She says; it's within my power to save you, because to the gods all things are possible, but I choose not to.

He could quite reasonably say several things at this point. It's not fair. You can't do that. It's against the rules.

I've repented, I meant it, you've got to forgive me, I'm entitled. He could quote scripture at me. He could remind me of the provisions of the Great Covenant. He could threaten me with lawyers. Or he could plead, beg, grovel.

He does none of the above.

Instead, he stares at me, as I stand there with my back to my own statue; he realises what's just happened, he understands. I should have forgiven him, but I've chosen not to. It's against the rules. It's unfair. Tough. I can do it, because I'm bigger than he is, and so much stronger. He understands strength, having always had it. He knows that when you're the strongest you can do whatever you like, and screw the rules.

He has his own rules, you see. And he abides by them.

"I SEE," HE said.

At that moment, for two pins I would've given him absolution, just for being a brave boy and a good little soldier. I had to struggle with myself and overcome the generous impulse.

"Good," I said.

He took a step back. He was still gazing at me. For a moment, I wasn't quite sure what was going on; then it dawned on me. He was exhibiting Faith. I nearly burst out laughing.

Forgive me; I don't mean to sound frivolous. But consider. The goddess appears to him, to tell him that she has rejected his prayer and condemned him, in violation of the Great Covenant. Is he angry? I'd have been, in his shoes. Livid. But no. He stands and gazes in adoration; because all his life he's wanted to believe, to have true faith; most of the time he sort of manages, but there are those terrible moments of doubt which he can't seem to shake off—you can't make yourself believe, just as you can't make yourself be two inches taller; it happens or it doesn't. Then, at this particular moment, he sees. Yes, Archias, there is a Goddess; she's real, she exists. True, she's just condemned him to Hell, but—

But he believes. Absolutely and without reservation. And Hell is a small price to pay.

They ask me sometimes, why do you bother with them? That's why. Because they never cease to amaze me.

MORTAL HUMANS HAVE asked me before now; what's it like, being a goddess?

I answer; I don't know. I've never been anything else.

They look at me. Naturally, they don't upbraid me for an unhelpful answer, which they feel sure is untrue and misleading. But they think; come off it, you're the Goddess, surely you know everything. I don't, of course.

I LEFT HIM and went out into the sunlight and fresh air. I'll be honest, I don't like my Temple very much. It's hard to put my finger on exactly why—the statue, yes, it's awful, the most blasphemous slab of marble in the universe, but I can put up with it. I just don't feel at home there, I suppose. The truth is, of course, that I have no home. I am unconfined, because I am unconfinable. I can't be contained by anything; I'm too big.

I'd been nothing if not scrupulously truthful. I was indeed hungry; ravenous. Mortal food doesn't seem to fill you up, somehow. It's all right, I suppose, but when you on honeydew have fed and drunk the milk of Paradise, a slice of bread and a sliver of leathery cheese doesn't go very far. Remembering who I was supposed to be, I walked across the square to a certain wine-shop-come-bakery where my kind were welcome. I didn't have any money aside from the big gold cartwheels that nobody can give change for, but some nice gentleman would be bound to buy me lunch.

Sure enough. I hadn't been there long enough to tie a shoelace when a man came up and sat down beside me. He was about twenty-three, very tall, big shoulders, slim waist, masses of curly golden hair and an impossibly handsome face. He gave me a big smile. Oh for crying out loud, I thought.

"Excuse me," he said, "but is this seat taken?"

I looked at him. He looked back at me. No flicker of recognition.

"Pol," I said, "it's me. Your sister."

A count of three during which he was incapable of speech. Then he turned all petulant. "What the hell are you doing here?"

"I'm hungry," I told him. "You can buy me lunch."

"Why should I?"

"You were just about to ask me if you could."

"I didn't realise—Oh, why not?" Short hesitation. "You won't tell Myrrhine, will you?"

My brother Polynices married Myrrhine, the daughter of the East Wind, for purely dynastic and geographical reasons. They don't get on. Fortunate, isn't it, that we as a race aren't nearly as omniscient as mortals think.

"I'm a cheap date," I reassured him. "The price of my silence is the house fish stew." He looked mildly relieved, so I added, "But she's going to find out one of these days, and then you'll be for it."

"I don't care," he lied. "You really eat that stuff?"

"You really have sex with mortal women? For *fun?*"

He shrugged. "When you're hungry, the house fish stew is better than nothing. You want bread with that?"

I nodded. "And grated cheese on top."

"You're weird." He wandered off to place the order, then came back. "You didn't answer my question," he said. "What are you doing here?"

"Administering divine justice," I told him.

"Ah." He looked at me. "Nice body."

"Oh get lost."

"No, really. Did you make it up, or is it copied from a real one? And if so, where does she live?"

Pol is strange. "This is a coincidence, isn't it?" I said. "They haven't sent you to check up on me?"

He yawned. "Don't flatter yourself." Then he looked at me a bit sideways and said, "Why? Are you up to something?"

"Me? Of course not."

We're dreadful liars in my family. I mean, we can deceive anybody about anything when we put our minds to it, because to the gods all things are possible. But we're dreadful liars. "Don't feel you have to tell me if you don't want to. After all, I'm only your brother."

"Why have I always got to be up to something?"

"Good question."

Some duly authorised officer of the wine-shop plonked down two bowls of the house fish stew and two wooden spoons. Pol gazed at his in mute bewilderment, while I tucked in.

"So," he said, "what gave me away? How did you recognise me?"

"For crying out loud, Pol."

"What?"

I gazed into his eyes. "You overdo it," I said.

"Really?"

"Use your eyes, Pol. Humans don't look like that."

"Really good looking humans do."

"Pol, you're wearing perfect teeth. *Perfect* teeth. Just stop and think for a moment, will you?"

He shrugged. "I don't get many complaints from the chicks."

The words he picks up. I recalled something someone had said to me. "You should be ashamed of yourself."

"Why?"

Good question. Excellent question. "Do you want that stew?"

"No."

I commandeered it and went on eating. "Father was asking about you," he said.

Ah. "Asking about me in what sense exactly?"

"Where you'd got to. What you're doing. You haven't been home in ages."

Not strictly true. I time my visits so as to coincide with the absences of members of my family. "I'm amazed he noticed."

"Of course he *noticed*."

"I'm amazed he took note."

(Valid distinction. He notices everything, naturally; the way you see everything in your field of vision, right out to the periphery. But you only look at what you're interested in. Same with hearing. He hears every mortals' prayer, but mostly he can't give a damn.)

"I think he's worried about something."

The chief culinary officer had been negligent in removing all the bones. One lodged in my throat; I dissolved it, but it takes a second. "What?"

Pol shrugged. "He doesn't confide in me."

"Ah well. He's Him. Everything that happens anywhere in the universe is officially his fault. He *ought* to be worried, all the time."

He speared a button mushroom out of my stew with a toothpick. "Are you up to something? Honestly?"

I sighed. "I interfere in the destinies of mortals," I said.

"I'll take that as a no."

LATER I WENT to visit Lord Archias in prison. I felt I owed him that much, but prisons depress me. I guess that's the point of them. They'd put him in a tower, with one of the best views in the City; looking out over the Horsefair, with its broad streets and brightly coloured awnings, across to the river and the majestic prospect of the Silver Mountains in the far distance. Lord Archias could gaze out of his narrow, barred window and reflect that, a couple of days ago, he'd owned most of what he could see.

"Oh," he said. "It's you."

I'd avoided all the tiresome formalities by walking in through the wall. "If you're busy," I said, "I could come back later."

He was sitting on a stone ledge that presumably functioned as a bed. "Yes," he said. "Come back in four days' time."

I frowned. "Your execution is in three days."

"Yes."

I was disappointed. Hurt, even. I turned to go, waiting to be called back. I wasn't, so I stopped. "I thought you had faith," I said.

"I did. I have." He shrugged. "Like they say, be careful what you wish for. I believe in you. But you're a complete shit."

"Brave words for a man on the brink of eternity."

"You're not going to save me."

"No," I said.

"Well, then. You're a shit."

I conjured a marble throne and sat down. "That's interesting," I said. "A man awaits execution, followed by eternity in perpetual torment. He knows he won't be forgiven. In the presence of the living goddess, he abuses her." I looked at him. "Is that usual?"

He laughed. "I don't think this sort of thing happens often enough for there to be a usual," he said.

"Sure," I said. "But you know more about human nature than I do. Is this what most mortals would do, in your shoes? Or are you exceptional in some way?"

He sighed. "Go fuck yourself," he said.

Disappointed, to put it mildly. Last time we were together, hell had been a small price to pay. Now; go fuck yourself. So volatile. So mutable. I'd hoped for better, from a mortal. "I'll pretend I didn't hear that," I said.

He yawned, lay down on the bench. It didn't look terribly comfortable. "What can I do for you?" he said. "I assume there's a reason why you're here."

"I wanted to see how you're getting on."

"Why?"

"Curiosity."

He turned his head and frowned at me. "Why won't you forgive me?" he said. "I repented. I was sincere."

"You hurt me."

He laughed. "That's impossible."

"You did. You damaged me. You inflicted on me an injury that can't be healed."

"Bullshit. To the gods, all things are possible."

"It's complicated. You wouldn't understand."

He shrugged. "What did I do that caused you irreparable harm?"

"You murdered Lysippus."

"True." He waited, then said, "So?"

"Lysippus the musician," I said.

He thought for a moment. "You're right," he said, "I remember now, he did write music. Songs and little fiddly bits for flute and strings." He looked up. "Is that important?"

Members of my family aren't often lost for words. I nodded.

"That's ridiculous," he said.

"To you, maybe."

"No, but it is. Lysippus was the third biggest land-owner in the Republic. He was a vicious, ambitious political animal. His family and mine have been feuding for twelve generations. He was my only real rival for the Consulate. He was about to stage a coup which would've thrown the Republic into chaos. Oh yes, and he was an atheist, which is rather ironic, don't you think." He stopped and looked down at his hands. "He was also my best friend. And my wife's lover."

If he was expecting me to say anything, he was disappointed.

"He was all that," he went on, "and I killed him. It was understandable, and probably necessary. It was my duty. It was also wrong. So I repented. I was sorry for what I'd done. Given my time over again, I wouldn't do it, and not just because of winding up in here." He breathed out slowly, then in again. "And now you're telling me I'm damned for all eternity because he wrote *songs*?"

"Very good songs," I said. "I liked them."

I'd upset him. "So fucking what?"

"So," I said, "when he died, his talent died with him. It was unique. There will be no more music like that, ever again. I love music. It's the only thing in the universe which I perceive to be—" I searched helplessly for the word. Stronger? Better? "The only thing beyond my power to command," I said.

He stared at me. "Surely not."

"Quite true, unfortunately," I told him. "I can inspire anyone I like with divine genius, but what they come up with will be, well, different. It'll be wonderful, but it won't be the music of Lysippus. That's all lost, gone for ever. Because of you."

"And that's—"

"Why I won't forgive you, yes."

He was stunned. "Why not just raise him from the dead, if it's such a big deal?"

I shook my head slowly.

"But to the gods—"

"Possible, yes. Allowed, no."

He considered me for a long time. "Balls," he said. "I don't believe you."

THERE, NOW. IF you can't trust the Goddess, who can you trust?

Faith is relative, and conditional. Or, if you prefer; just because you believe in me doesn't necessarily mean you believe me. Why, after all, do you tell the truth? Because it's the right thing to do, or for fear you'll be found out? Or because you simply want to impart accurate information?

To the gods all things are possible. So we can lie through our teeth, if we want to. Sometimes, though, we don't want to. By the same token, there are other things we can do but choose not to. Even if we really, really want to.

But let's not go there.

HE'D ANNOYED ME so much I went home.

Is there any point trying to describe something that only a tiny handful of conscious minds in the universe are capable of understanding; and who need no description, since they live there, always have, always will?

Mind you, people have tried. In the cloudy heights (this is one of my favourites) dwell the gods; War Hall is their home. They are spirits of light, and Light-Spirit rules them. Well; that's close enough for government work. Home for me is a space almost big enough to be comfortable in, except that I have to share it with a dozen members of my family, as big as me or bigger. Fact; some of us are bigger than others. My father, for example, is the biggest of the big; he's *huge*. Query, in fact, whether there's any limit to his size. Answer (probably); if he wants there to be one, there is.

Home as I perceive it is a vast castle, bare stone walls, bare stone floor. The dominant colour is sandstone red.

The only light slides in sideways through high, narrow windows, or gushes out of hearths. Furniture happens when I want it, then falls away in clouds of dust—indeed; home as I perceive it is dirty, undusted, unkempt. The doors creak, because the hinges are three parts seized. None of the windows open. How the others perceive it I neither know nor care, but I should imagine it's cleaner and more cheerful.

The generally accepted form of communication in my family is melodrama. I see us as actors performing in a huge auditorium; so far away that unless we shout and make huge, over-the-top gestures, we can't be seen or heard. All about perspective, I guess. I don't like my family, and I'm not comfortable talking about them.

Father was in his study. I perceive it as a freezing cold stone box, impossibly high ceiling, dark, gloomy, every surface stuffed and crammed with piles of unsorted books and papers; himself slouched in a massive ebony chair, feet up on the desk, book on his knees, not reading. He looked up and scowled at me. "Where have you been?"

"Out," I said. "You wanted to see me."

"No," he replied, "I wanted to know where you'd got to."

"Fine," I said. "Can I go now?"

"Shut up and sit down."

To the gods all things are possible, but some things aren't easy, such as finding somewhere to sit in all that mess. I pushed a sheaf of papers off a chair onto the floor, and perched. "What?"

He squinted through what I perceived as gold-rimmed spectacles at a bit of paper. "You refused a mortal's prayer," he said. "Why?"

"I felt like it."

"You don't deny it, then."

"No."

"You felt like it."

"Yes."

"It was a properly constituted prayer, correctly phrased and made with sincere intent."

"So?"

He sighed. "It's all a question," he said, "of how it looks from the road, as my father used to say. When a mortal prays in correct form and we don't answer, it looks bad. Brings us into disrepute. You must see that, surely."

Please note; Father is head of the family because he bound Grandpa in adamantine chains and imprisoned him at the centre of the earth, where presumably he still is. Quoting Grandpa's folksy sayings cuts no ice with me. "Yes, and I don't give a damn."

"That's a rather irresponsible attitude."

"What are you going to do about it?"

IN OUR FAMILY, what-are-you-going-to-do-about-it is like a great city in the middle of settled, fertile countryside. There are a great many roads, leading from countless small villages, and sooner or later they all lead to the city;

no matter where you start from, here is where you arrive. We still go through the motions—accusation, defence, rational debate, argument, counter-argument, rebuttal, counter-rebuttal, pre-emptive defensive strike—but there is and can only be one culmination; what are you going to do about it?

Well; there's two things he can do:

Throw the offender off the ramparts of Heaven. He or she will fall for three days, and on landing will sink a crater a mile wide and fill the air with a dust-cloud that takes a week to settle. After that, he or she will spend a certain time—hundreds or thousands of years—chained to a mountain being gnawed by eagles, or something of the sort, until Father finds he needs him (or her) back home as an ally in the latest family civil war, or until some mortal hero shoots the eagle and cuts the chain, under the fond misapprehension that members of our family understand about gratitude; or

Nothing.

"SPARE ME THE drama, please," he said wearily. "But don't you agree? It's exactly the sort of thing that makes us unpopular. And you can see why, you of all people. You're the one who's so mad keen on *understanding* them."

To the gods all things are possible, so I kept my temper. "Wanting to understand them isn't the same as giving a stuff what they think," I said. "You should know that," I added, "of all people."

He glowered at me. "I'm asking you as a personal favour to me."

"What?"

"You heard me. Just for once, remember who you are. We have *responsibilities*."

HE'D GOT ME. Quite true. Just as a man has a responsibility to his dog, or a little girl to her dolls. Note, by the way, that I can only explain this concept by reference to mortal analogies. In my family, we don't have the vocabulary.

Didn't mean I had to like it, though. I had no choice—he'd asked nicely; that's pretty heavy stuff, in my family—but what I did have was a wide degree of room for interpretation.

Lord Archias was asleep. Imagine that; in twenty-four hours they were going to string him up like onions, and he was sleeping. I prodded him awake. He rolled over and scowled at me.

"Go away," he said.

Playing right into my hands; I was perfectly within my rights to blow him away straight to hell for talking to me like that. "If you want," I said. "I came here to forgive you, but—"

I was expecting, and hoping, that he'd collapse, go all to pieces, start grovelling. Instead he frowned. "You're playing games, aren't you?"

"Don't annoy me," I warned him.

He grinned at me. "You were always going to forgive me," he said, "you've got to, it's the rules. But you made me believe you were going to let me be damned anyway. Playing games."

"Careful," I said. "That's blasphemy."

"So's what you're doing."

"Incorrect," I said. "A goddess can't blaspheme, like water can't get wet."

"Technicality. What you're doing is basically the same thing. You're making a mockery of what is sacred. You're pissing on the Covenant."

I took three long deep breaths to calm myself down. "I should burn you down where you stand," I said.

"Yes," he replied casually. "You should. Really, it's your duty. But I know you aren't going to."

"Is that right."

"Yes. Because you want something from me. Otherwise yes, I'd be ashes by now." He looked at me down far more nose than any circumstances could ever justify. "You're pathetic," he said.

THIS BUSINESS OF the Covenant.

A mortal who thought he was really clever once posed the question; can God create a rock so heavy that he can't lift it? Clearly he knew nothing about my family. It's the sort of thing we do to each other all the time. Because to us all things are possible, we get our kicks, and pass the endless, dreary time, creating rocks the others can't lift; just to spite them, because we can. As witness my father and me. The rock I can't lift is when he asks me nicely.

But the Covenant—Do you really think we'd sign up to something that actually restricted us, confined our freedom of choice and action? And for what in return? No, we abide by it because it pleases us to do so. And if it doesn't please—Well.

(Pol reckons we abide by the Covenant because, being infinite, at some level we crave containment; for the same reason that, being imperishable, insensitive to cold and heat and definitively waterproof, nevertheless we sleep indoors, under a roof. Among his other titles and portfolios, Pol is God of Wisdom. I think that says it all.)

"You do realise," I said, "that since I got here, you've forfeited your right to clemency under the Covenant at least three times. Are you stupid, or what?"

"Maybe I don't want clemency."

"Don't be ridiculous."

"Maybe I don't want it from you."

I don't gasp, but if I did, I would've. "I think I'll go away and come back later," I said. "When you've had time to think."

"I thought you might say that," he said. "I expect you'll leave it right to the very last minute, when they're putting the rope round my neck." He yawned. "Play your games if you want to. It's all right. I know you'll save me. I have faith."

"Do you now."

He nodded. "I know you want something from me. Yea, though I walk through the valley of the shadow of Death, if you want something from me, I know I'll be just fine. Well? Am I right?"

"Let's wait to the very last moment and find out."

But he just smiled at me, confident, cocky. Well; it's not often an immortal gets a chance to try something new. So I decided to be a good loser.

"It's all right," I said. "You've made your point. Let's get down to cases. Yes, I'm prepared to grant you clemency. Your life will be spared. More to the point, the sentence of eternal damnation will be lifted. Suspended, anyway. But there are conditions."

He looked so smug, I could've sworn we must be related. "Good heavens," he said. "Fancy that."

"You're going to get another chance. If you can prove that you truly feel remorse for what you've done, you will be forgiven and the slate will be wiped clean. If not, you'll find yourself back here. Do you understand?"

"Perfectly." He waited, then folded his hands in his lap and said, "What do you want?"

As I LEFT the prison, I tripped over an old beggar sitting on the steps. He was a horrible creature; one eye, one withered arm, one leg missing from the knee down.

"Bless you, sweetheart," he called out—I'd just trodden on his good hand. "God bless you and keep you."

The irony appealed to me, so I gave him a coin, one of the two I had on me, and walked on. "Are you mad?" he called out after me. I stopped and turned round.

"Five gulden," he said, with the coin lying flat on his outstretched palm. "Have you no idea of the value of money?"

I sighed. "Dad," I said.

He stood up. The absence of his left leg didn't hinder him. "Five gulden," he said, "is a fortune to these people, it's the price of a farm. Even I know that. You can't just go flinging it around. First thing you know, they'll have galloping inflation."

"I earned that," I told him. "By the sweat of my—"

"I know you did." He scowled at me. "Well? Did you forgive him, like I told you?"

"Conditionally."

"What's that supposed to mean?"

"Dad," I said, "sit down. People are staring."

He sat down quickly. "Conditionally," he said. "What sort of condition?"

"It's perfectly fair," I told him. "Just like in the Covenant. Sometimes, when they've been really bad or you don't believe they're truly sincere, you make them prove themselves. More to the point," I went on quickly, "how dare you come checking up on me like this? It's insulting."

A passer-by dropped a two-groschen in Father's hat. "Bless you, sir, bless you. The ship you thought was lost will come safe to port in two days' time." The man gawped at him for a moment, then hurried away. "Charity is good," Father said, when I raised an eyebrow at him. "It enriches the giver as well as the receiver. We ought to encourage it. And I wouldn't need to check up on you if you did as you're told. What condition?"

NOW, THEN. ABOUT me.

I was born—Sorry, I'll have to be careful here. Wars have been fought and men have been burnt alive over differences in nuance in accounts of how and when I was born. For obvious reasons, I'm reluctant to endorse any one version as against the others. It's awkward. I love talking about myself, but one has a responsibility to the weak-minded and the faithful.

I live at home. Not all of us do. My uncle Thaumastus lives at the bottom of the sea. Likewise my aunt Feralia, who hardly ever leaves her tastefully appointed palace in the Underworld. They claim they have to be on site at all times for the proper performance of their duties. I don't believe them. I think they saw an excuse to get away from the rest of us, and grabbed it with both hands. I can make no such claim. Love, laughter and joy are everywhere, as Father constantly reminds me, and home is centrally located, in easy reach of all civilised nations. I have a room of my own, if you can call it that, but we've never been great ones for knocking on doors in our family, so I might as well sleep in the Great Hall for all the privacy I can expect. I own the clothes I stand up in, when I wear a body. That's all. What does a god want with possessions, Father's always saying. He's quite right, of course; though that doesn't stop him hoarding all sorts of junk in the treasury of his temple at Blachernae. He thinks we don't know about that. The idiot.

Ah well. Naked I came into the world, and what's the use of owning things when you're bound to outlast them? If I had a diamond necklace, contact with my soft white breast would wear the stones away in no time. Anyway, what good are things? No attire or ornament could possibly make me any more beautiful than I am already. I do no work, so I need no tools. Nothing in the world, not even being thrown off the ramparts of heaven and digging a mile-wide impact crater, could conceivably harm me, so armour and weapons would be pointless. Cutlery and tableware; we eat with our fingers in our family. We need nothing, have no use for anything. Therefore, we have nothing. Lucky us.

Correction; we do have something. We have each other.

Lucky, lucky us.

"I won't do it," Pol said. "Absolutely and definitely not. No. No way."

I smiled at him. "I'll take that as a yes."

"You're mad," he said. "Anyway, Dad'll never agree."

"Actually—"

He stared at me. "You're joking."

"He thinks it's a splendid idea," he said.

"But he can't. It's—it's *wrong*."

"Define *wrong*. I was always brought up to believe it means contrary to the will of the gods. Therefore—"

"It's wrong," he repeated. "It's one of the things we don't do. You know that."

I widened the smile. Not for nothing was I appointed Goddess of Charm in the last reshuffle. "Yes, but it's not us doing it, is it? That's the point."

"Oh come on," he whined, "that's just sophistry. No way he can do it without your help. Or mine. Therefore, to all intents and purposes—"

"Pol," I said. "Please. Pretty please."

He winced as though I'd slapped his face. "It's a bit extreme, isn't it? All this, for some mortal."

"It's not for him," I said, a bit too quickly. "It's about ethics. Morality. It's about the meaning of restitution. We have a duty to teach mortals how to behave."

He gave me his sad look. "What are you up to?" he said.

"For crying out loud, I'm not up to anything. Why does everyone always assume I'm up to something? Believe it or not, my entire life isn't spent in devising malign schemes of impenetrable complexity."

"True. From time to time you sleep."

"Shut up, Pol. And you're going to help me. Father says so."

He raised his hands as though in silent prayer. "I give up," he said. "This family is impossible. Just don't blame me if it all ends in disaster."

"Pol," I said, "don't be silly. What could possibly go wrong?"

LORD ARCHIAS WAS shocked. "You're joking."

"No."

He tried to back away, but he was up against the cell wall already. "It's impossible. You can't do that."

"To the gods—"

He shook his head. "Not that," he said. "It's specifically excluded, everyone knows that. To the gods all things are possible, but they can't raise the dead. It's— it's *fundamental*."

I sighed. "You poor dear," I said. "You obviously don't know the first thing about what we can and can't do. We're the gods, we can do anything."

"Including—?"

I nodded. "We choose not to," I said, "most of the time. But we have the discretion. Besides," I added, "we're not going to. You are."

He gave me a look of pure distilled revulsion. "I can't."

"With a little help," I said. "Or maybe you don't want to. Maybe you aren't sincerely remorseful after all. In which case—"

"That's not the point."

I grinned. The words had come out all in a rush. He was afraid. I'd beaten him. "If you sincerely regret killing Lysippus the musician, you must want him to be alive again."

"I do."

"Fine. Then prove it. Go to the Kingdom of the Dead and bring him back."

Directly behind his head was that wonderful view of the city and the mountains. I looked past them, across the Middle Sea, through the dense forests of the Mesoge, over the White Desert to the Holy Mountain, and met Father's eye. *I hope you know what you're doing,* I lip-read.

"There's no such place," he said. "There is no Kingdom of the Dead, it's a human myth."

I raised an eyebrow. "Is it really."

"Yes. Logically, it must be."

"Do explain."

He looked up at me angrily. "The dead don't come back," he said. "Therefore, all and any accounts of the Kingdom of the Dead circulating among mortals can't be based on eyewitness testimony. But the traditional accounts are full of lurid and picaresque detail. They must therefore be lies. Therefore there is no Kingdom of the Dead. Logic."

"Mphm. It exists. I've been there. It's run by my aunt. She's not the nicest person ever, but compared to the rest of my relatives she's not too bad. And you can take your logic and shove it."

He breathed out slowly. "This is ridiculous," he said.

He was getting on my nerves. "Do you have to make a fuss about every damn thing?"

He raised his hands in surrender. "There is a Kingdom of the Dead," he said, "because you say so. If I don't go there, I die and suffer eternal torment. The way I see it, I've got as much choice as a nail." He looked up at me. "Well?"

"I think you've got the gist of it."

He nodded. "That's mortals for you," he said. "We can be trained to perform simple tasks."

I ADMIRED HIM for that remark, though probably I read too much into it. But consider the relationship between gods and men as roughly analogous to that between the man and his dog. The virtues the man ordains for his dog—unquestioning obedience, biting intruders, peeing outdoors, fetching sticks—aren't the qualities that you look for in a good human; they're dog virtues. The dog feels moral outrage because it brings back the stick, and then the man throws it away again; idiotic, irrational behaviour. But the man throws the stick to exercise the dog and keep it healthy; and the dog, of course, will never be able to understand all that, because it's just a dog. The dog shouldn't presume to pass judgement on the purpose or the merit of the simple tasks it's trained to perform. From down there, they pass all understanding. From up here; well, it's just a dog. It's not like it's a *person*.

"FIRST," I SAID, "we'll have to clear up this mess you've got yourself into."

I made it sound easy. Actually, it wasn't as straight-forward as all that. To put Lord Archias back in the fortunate circumstances he enjoyed before he committed the murder I could reverse time, but then I'd have to edit and redact three months of history, every connection, every consequence: I can do that, but it's awkward, fiddly work, involving co-operation with other members of my family. I chose a simpler approach.

The cell door blew open and crashed against the wall. A jailer ran up, sword drawn. "It's all right," I told him, and smiled. He backed away, looking foolish, and apologised. I led Archias down the long spiral staircase, with guards and warders skipping out of our way as we went. The porter on the main gate was delighted to shoot back the bolts and let us through. We walked briskly up Horsefair to the Council Chamber, where the sentries let us pass without a murmur. As luck would have it the Council was in session. We walked in; I cleared my throat. They all stopped talking. I explained that although Lord Archias was guilty as charged of the murder of Count Lysippus, it'd be nice if they pardoned him and restored all his properties, titles and privileges, effective immediately. They were only too happy to agree; carried unanimously.

"YOU CAN BUY me lunch," I said. "As a thank-you."

I chose a wine-shop I like in the Arches. They do the most delicious sea bass.

"Why use raw power," I explained, "when you can get the job done so much more easily with charm? Like pigs. You can drag the pig into the cart with a rope round its neck, because you're stronger. Or you can put a few cabbage-stalks on the tailgate, and he'll happily go in of his own accord."

He looked at me over his wine-glass. "But you could drag him," he said. "You just choose not to."

"For convenience," I said. "To the gods all things are possible, but some things are easier than others. Did I mention, I'm the Goddess of Charm?"

"Really."

"Among other things. It's significant that charm has two meanings. It really is a kind of magic."

Archias nodded. "A man sits in the market square," he said. "He's got a sign up, *Magic Performed Here*. Someone stops and asks him, what kind of magic? Well, says the magician, pay me two gold coins, I'll use a magic talisman to make a perfect stranger do exactly what I tell him to. So the magician leads his customer into a baker's shop, and he hands the shopkeeper a penny and says, Give me a loaf of bread." He shrugged. "That kind of magic."

"Yes."

"Ah. Are we going to charm the Queen of the Dead into letting Lysippus go?"

"You can try."

"I don't do charm."

Not strictly true, though I suspect he didn't realise that was what he was doing. "You'll think of something, I'm sure," I said. "A resourceful man like you."

He sighed. "All right," he said. "If the Kingdom of the Dead is an actual place, where is it?"

"Beyond the Portals of the Sunset," I said, "on the far edge of the Great White Desert, at the place where the River of Lost Souls passes under the Bridge of Forgetfulness." He gave me a blank look. "I'll draw you a map."

"Which country is it in? Can we ride there, or do we need a ship? Are we at war with the people whose land we have to cross? Can I drink the water? Do I have to get a visa?"

I told him where we were going. Forgive me if I leave out the specifics; classified. "At this time of year? I'll freeze."

"Actually, the White Desert is the hottest place on Earth."

He'd gone pale. "This is going to be a logistical nightmare," he said. "We'll need wagons, mules, drivers, porters, a large armed escort—"

I shook my head. "You can't take anyone else with you," I said. "Not other mortals, anyway."

"Why the hell not?"

"They're not the ones who need to redeem themselves. Only you."

"For pity's sake, woman." He realised what he'd said and glanced at me. I shrugged. "For pity's sake," he repeated. "In order to cross mountains, forests and deserts I'm going to need food and water, far more than I can carry. And a tent, and climbing gear, and an axe for firewood, and money, and weapons. Or are you going to magic all that out of thin air whenever I need it?"

"In your dreams," I said. "This is a penance, not a holiday."

"Why do I get the feeling you haven't thought this through? I'll need changes of clothing, spare boots, rope, accurate and detailed maps, a portable stove and cooking gear. Don't just shake your head like that, I'm human. I need things."

"No," I said. "You just think you do. All you actually need is for me to forgive you your terrible sin, because if I don't you're going to die. Everything else is just would-be-nice."

SOME PEOPLE JUST won't listen. The rest of the day was incredibly dull. We had to go to see his bankers, so he could draw out money. Then we had a dreary trudge round the city while he tried on about ninety pairs of boots, ditto travelling cloaks, hats, thornproof leggings, ultra-lightweight oilskin trousers, whatever. The only points of interest for me were the gadgets he insisted on looking at; folding knives with six different blades and a spoon, collapsible tents that doubled as stoves and dog-sleighs, hats with button-down compartments for fish-hooks, flints and tinder. The ingenuity of it all; the idea that mortals can to some degree compensate for their lack of strength and endurance by the judicious use of *things*. Buy this hat or that four-in-one shovel/water-flask/boar-spear/walking-stick and you can hike your way up the pyramid of hierarchies until you're practically a god. Poor darlings. If only it were possible.

He kept it to the bare minimum (so he said) but by nightfall he was struggling along under a hundred and twenty pounds dead weight, and with every step he took he clanked like a dozen buckets. "Satisfied?" I asked him.

"No."

"You should be. You've redistributed a considerable amount of wealth and provided for the families of hard-working artisans. And when you get sick of lugging all that junk around and dump it by the roadside, I expect the poor villagers who find it will be able to sell it for good money."

He stopped, and leaned against a wall. "Clarify something for me, please."

"Sure."

"If I die while trying to carry out this idiotic quest, will I escape eternal damnation?"

"I don't know."

"You don't know. For crying out loud—"

"I hadn't considered the point," I said. "I mean, it's hard to me to understand. I was sort of assuming that of course you'd make it there, because for me it's a two-minute stroll. But you mortals are so frail, you drop dead from the silliest things."

He was breathing hard through his nose. "Consider it now."

41

"Don't rush me," I said. "There are arguments on both sides. How dare you try and bounce me into making up my mind?"

He groaned, and shifted the weight of his Feather-Lite combination rucksack/tent/parasol/coracle. "When you decide," he said, "please tell me. I'd like to know if I've got the option of just giving up and dying."

"Sissy," I said.

THERE ARE SEVERAL different ways for members of my family to take on human form. We can weave a cloud of illusion—mortals look at us and see what we want them to—or we can create and inhabit an actual physical body. I tend to favour the latter. I've always loved dressing up, ever since I was a little girl, and besides, if you want to understand a man, I always say, you need to walk a mile on his feet. I take pains to equip myself with bodies that are fit, strong and healthy as well as radiantly beautiful. The body I'd selected for this job was about as close to functional perfection as human flesh and blood can get. Height-to-weight ratio, metabolic rate and lung capacity were optimal, the muscles and tendons perfectly tuned and supple, and I'd fuelled it with the full recommended daily intake of vitamins, proteins and carbohydrates. But next day, after nine hours or so of walking—

"Keep up, can't you?"

"I've got a stone in my shoe," I lied.

"You're dawdling."

"I've got shorter legs than you."

"So make them longer."

I'd toyed with the idea, but I was pretty sure he'd notice. So, when he was looking the other way, I dispensed with the flesh and blood, resumed my usual form and clothed it in an illusion of what I'd been looking like all day. Much better. I could float along beside him comfortably without getting splints in my shins. "You've changed," he said suspiciously. "There's something different about you."

"I've done my hair. How much further is it?"

"Not long now."

"Let me see the map."

Boring. A waste of time. They have so little time, yet they don't seem concerned about frittering it away on repetitive activities such as walking. If I had to move at their pace I'd die of frustration.

"You've got the map upside down," he said.

"Makes no difference. I can read non-relativistically." He pulled a sad face. "I don't need a fixed viewpoint," I explained.

"But you do need a map."

"I'm trying to enter into the spirit of things."

"Admit it," he said. "You're tired."

Well, it was very perceptive of him. "Yes," I said. "My mortal body can't keep up with me."

"Fine." He took off his cloak and spread it on the grass. "Have a rest."

"No, thank you."

"Have a rest," he repeated. "Look, we'll cover far more ground if we rest for half an hour and then proceed for three hours at three miles an hour than if we drag on at two and a bit for three and a half hours. Simple mathematics."

I sat down. It felt wonderful. "You're not tired," I said.

"No. I'm used to walking."

I thought for a moment. "You could've insisted we carry on, thereby causing me pain and humiliation. But you didn't. Why?"

He shrugged. "It wouldn't have been a nice thing to do."

"But politically, in the power-struggle between us, you'd have scored points. You'd have allowed me to make a fool of myself, thereby securing a slight edge."

He gave me a curious look. "I don't think in those terms. Do you?"

"Always."

He gathered some dry sticks, lit a fire, boiled some water and made jasmine tea. My feet were killing me—my real ones. As I said, I'd got rid of the flesh-and-blood ones earlier; but the ache somehow lingered, just as humans claim they feel pain in long-since-amputated limbs. I pulled off the illusion of boots and wriggled my toes till the feeling started to come back.

He was looking at me. "What?" I said.

"Nothing."

He was lying. "What?" I repeated.

"When you're ready," he said, "we'd better get going. We've still got a long way to go."

I shrugged, and suffused my entire being with strength and vigour. "Fine," I said. "I was just giving you a chance to rest."

Up in the sky, my uncle Actis was about four-fifths through the daily grind. I hoped he hadn't seen me, but when I looked closely, he winked and waved. Clown.

"You shouldn't do that."

"What?"

"Stare straight into the sun. You'll hurt your eyes."

"Sweet of you to be concerned," I said.

The collar of the illusion of a coat was chafing the back of my neck—yes, all my imagination, but a chafing sensation is none the less uncomfortable when it's all in your head—so I peeled it off. He screamed, and dropped to his knees.

"Oh," I said. "Sorry." I created the illusion of a long-sleeved blouse.

"You stupid bloody woman," he was shrieking. "I'm blind. I can't see."

"Careless of me," I said, restoring his sight. "It's all right. No harm done."

He opened his eyes, rubbed them and groaned. "You just don't get it, do you? You're like a giant in a playground. You never look where you're putting your feet."

"I said I'm sorry."

He was massaging his forehead. "Headache?"

"Yes. No, don't do *anything*," he snapped, "just leave me alone, all right?"

"Now you're being childish."

"This is hopeless," he said. He struggled to his feet, then sat down on the ground. "No offence," he said, "but how would it be if we split up and I met you at wherever this place is we're going?"

"Don't be stupid. You'll never get there on your own."

"I can try."

"You'll die," I told him. "And if you die before you've fulfilled your penance, you'll suffer eternal torment. Probably," I added. "At any rate, it's not worth the risk."

He sighed. "I don't think I can stand any more of this."

"What?"

"Being with you."

STICKS AND STONES can't break my bones, but words sure can hurt me.

Words, in fact, are the only things that can hurt us, in our family. It hit me like—well, like the ground, I suppose; except that when one of us gets hurled from the ramparts of heaven, it's the ground that takes the heavy damage. I was so shocked I couldn't bear to stay there any more. With a thought, I soared back through the clouds, to where I always go when I'm upset; which is silly, because that's where nearly everything that upsets me happens.

"Hello," I called out. "I'm home."

Mother was in the Lesser Great Hall. I perceive it as a bleak, freezing cold hexagonal chamber at the far end of the house, with the back wall forming a huge picture window looking out on the Eastern Sea. She looked at me. "What are you doing here?" she said. "Aren't you supposed to be doing something?"

She was weaving. It's supposed to be the destinies of men, but I think it's just something she does to pass the time. Could be both, of course. "I needed a break."

"Really."

"That mortal just insulted me."

"Poor baby."

"He said he couldn't stand being with me."

She clicked her tongue. "Well," she said.

"What's that supposed to mean?"

A silence can be more eloquent than a million words. "What?" I demanded.

"That's mortals for you," she said. "No tact."

Coming from her, it was one of the most outrageous statements ever made. "Tact," I repeated. "You agree with him, don't you?"

"Of course not. Don't be silly."

"You do. You think I'm unpleasant to be with."

"Sweetheart." She wasn't looking at me. "You're my daughter and I love you. I want you to know that."

Terrible things happen when we get angry. Not to us, naturally. "But?"

She took just a little bit too long over choosing her words. "I've had plenty of time to get used to you," she said.

TIME. THE T word, in our house.

A mortal stands on the same hilltop every night and looks at the sky. To him, it appears that the stars are moving. All wrong, of course. The stars don't move; it's the Earth. (Sorry, didn't you know that? Oops. Forget I spoke)

It's the same with us and Time. We don't change. Things move past us, but we're fixed. I think I may have been young once, for twenty years, the blink of an eye; it was over so quick I didn't notice and certainly can't remember. I shall never be older than I am now, except in a dressing-up body. Of course I can look like anybody or anything I want, to anyone else; I can't see myself, for obvious reasons, except in a mirror or a glass darkly, and I never bother. Everybody and everything else blossoms and flourishes like leaves on a tree, and withers and perishes, but naught changeth me; so what would be the point?

Pol once said something interesting. If you don't travel, you don't arrive.

So, yes; my mother and my father, my brothers, sisters, uncles and aunts have all had plenty of time to get used to me. And even now, they can't stand me for more than five minutes. Am I really that bad?

"No," my mother said.

There were tears in my eyes. "You're just saying that."

"You're really not that bad," she said, "compared to the rest of us. No worse."

"No better?"

She snapped her fingers and the Loom of Destiny vanished. "This is all because you've been spending time with mortals," she said. "It doesn't do anyone any good. Look at Pol. All those dreadful mortal females. It makes him sulky and sarcastic."

"No better than any of the others?"

She shrugged. "What's so special about being better?" she said. "It's not like they give prizes for it."

I looked at her for quite some time. Then I said; "Thank you. That's all I needed to know."

"Is it? Did I say something clever?"

I nodded. "Purely by accident. I think I'll go now."

I could feel her relax. "It's not that I don't like having you home," she said. "It's just—"

"Yes."

She smiled at me. "I'm glad we understand each other."

"You're back," he said.

The T thing again. Three weeks had passed, in his timescale, since I stormed off in my huff. Since then he'd traversed four hundred miles of impossibly difficult terrain—towering mountain passes, impenetrable jungles, rivers in spate, fever-haunted marshes. Along the way he'd acquired two mules, laden with supplies and equipment. I vanished them irritably. He looked at the space where they'd been, and sighed.

"Against the rules," I said.

"No. The rule was, no porters or other humans."

"The rule changed."

"Ah."

He looked round to see what he'd got left. I glared at him, but he didn't notice. "You've got on fine without me, by the look of it."

That got his attention. "It's been hell," he growled at me. "I nearly died three times. I got swept away crossing a river, I lost my footing climbing a sheer cliff and ended up trapped in a crevasse, and I trod in quicksand."

"You're looking well on it."

"A caravan of No Vei heard me screaming, and they pulled me out. They fed me and gave me new clothes, since I'd lost absolutely everything. When I told them what I was trying to do, they told me I must be mad and gave me two mules laden with supplies." He paused. "I assume you're going to tell me that was all you, watching over me."

I'd been about to. "I knew you could look after yourself," I said. "For the easy stages of the journey."

Another sigh. "Did you have to take everything?"

"You won't need things now I'm back," I said. "You'll have me instead."

HE'D LET HIS hair grow long. It suited him.

He'd lost all the maps in the quicksand, of course, so I had to tell him the way. I have to concede, I didn't exactly cover myself in glory in my capacity as navigator. Things look different from the air—gradients, for example, and depths of rivers and thickness of ice, and you don't tend to notice whether or not there are bridges, or if the green bits are grassland or swamp. "You could fly us over that," he said, as we stood staring up at a vertical cliff-face I'd somehow overlooked. "Go on. It'd be easy as pie."

"Get thee behind me," I told him. "You have to do this, or it won't count."

"I'm an accomplished rock-climber," he said. "You're the one who keeps getting into difficulties."

True. But that's what the rope is *for*. I'd told him, go on, cut it, let me fall, but he insisted on hauling me up. I broke a fingernail.

"I'm a quick learner," I said. "We won't have any trouble this time."

"I hope not. Have you any idea how heavy you are?"

"Don't be idiotic. I'm insubstantial. I weigh practically nothing."

He looked at me and pulled a particularly irritating grin. "If you say so," he said. "Look, why don't you fly, and I'll meet you at the top?"

ACTUALLY, A VERY good question. I was, after all, accompanying him—which I could do in relative comfort, using my god-given faculties. Where this notion of sharing every aspect of the human experience had crept in, I wasn't sure. It wasn't in the original plan, but now it seemed to be of the essence of the enterprise. Ah well. What fun is a game if you can't change the rules as you go along?

We started to climb the cliff. He was right; he really was very good at it. We weren't roped together this time, because of course he'd lost the rope, and his spiky things you bash into the rock, and all the rest of the gear. I cheated just a little bit by reducing my body weight to that of a small feather.

About two-thirds of the way up, he grabbed hold of a ledge above his head and put his weight on it, and it crumbled and gave way. He scrabbled madly with his feet, but the soles of his boots slipped off the smooth surface of the cliff, and there wasn't another handhold in reach. He screamed, and fell.

What happened next is a bit of a blur; the next thing I remember clearly is touching down with both feet on the goat-cropped grass on the top of the cliff, and gently putting him down, as though he was made of glass.

He'd closed his eyes. He opened them and looked at me. The palms of his hands had been cut to ribbons, and there was a three-inch gash down his left cheek. I don't think he was aware of them, so I healed them before he noticed.

"Thank you," he said.

"See? Didn't I tell you? You do need me after all."

His eyes narrowed. "It was you," he said.

"I saved you, yes."

"You made the rock crumble under my hand. So you could rescue me."

I was so stunned I forgot to be angry. "No," I said, "I didn't. It was an accident. The rock was loose."

"I don't believe you."

"Really, it's true."

He got painfully to his feet. "Isn't there something in scripture about a providence in the fall of a sparrow? I don't think accidents happen when you're around."

"It was an accident, for crying out loud."

He shook his head. "Nice try. Presumably the crevasse and the quicksand were you as well. Proving to me I couldn't manage on my own."

"I wasn't *there*."

"You're everywhere, it says so in the Good Book."

"It's not true."

"Ah. So scripture tells lies, just like you. I'm not in the least surprised."

"I hate you," I said.

"You know, I'd sort of gathered that. Ever since I prayed to you in the Temple and you wouldn't forgive me."

"Drop dead."

He went white as a sheet, until he was certain he was still alive. "Figure of speech," I said. "I can do them, you know." I gave him my sincere look. "Really and truly, I didn't crumble the rock. It was an accident."

He had that wary look, like a dog that's been kicked and doesn't trust humans any more. He backed away a couple of steps, keeping his eyes on me all the time. "What?" I said. "What's the matter now?"

"You could've killed me."

"Don't be silly. I told you, it was just a figure of speech."

"But it needn't have been."

He'd lost me. "What?"

"You could've meant it. You could have ordered me to drop dead, and I'd have died."

I shrugged. "To the gods all things are possible, yes, big deal. What about it?"

"What would've happened then?"

I couldn't see what he was getting at. "You'd have been dead."

"Yes. And what would've happened to you?"

"Me?"

"Answer the question."

I turned away. "We need to get going," I said. "It's three miles due west, then we follow a sheep-track down into the valley. There's fresh water."

"Answer the question."

I still had my back to him. "All right," I said. "I'd have been sorry. And sad. But since I never had the slightest intention—"

"Nothing."

"You what?"

"Nothing would've happened to you," he said. "Nothing at all. You kill a man, you take a life, you shrug and move on. It could just be a whim, or a flash of pique. You lose your temper for less than a second, and that's that. No consequences."

"Not necessarily," I said. "That's getting into the whole business of predestination. I mean, if you were destined to do something important, like found a city or start a war, and you die before your time, then obviously there's consequences."

"No consequences," he said, "to you. Personally."

I had to turn round. "No," I said. "I suppose not."

He nodded slowly. "And then there's me," he said. "For twenty years, ever since we were children, Lysippus was the proverbial thorn in my flesh. He was bigger and older than me, he made me eat worms. His estate was next to mine; he was always breaking down fences, cutting my timber, leaving gates open. In politics, whichever side I was on, he was on the other side. He cheated me in business deals. He seduced my wife."

"I thought he was supposed to be your best friend."

"He was." He turned his head away. "He did it—Oh, I don't know. Mostly I think it was just teasing, counting coup. He liked to get me really angry, and then laugh at me. I think he really loved me, in his own way, like a brother. You know, like cats that scratch you? She only does it because she likes you?"

It sounded just a bit too much like my own family for comfort. "Humans," I said.

"Yes, maybe. We're not perfect. Me, I stuck it for twenty years, because he was my friend. I forgave him, over and over and over again. Then, when I came home and found him and Rhodope in our bed, I knew I couldn't stand it any longer." He shrugged. "And the moment he was dead, I was sorry. I knew I'd done the wrong thing."

"A bit late for that."

"Absolutely. I couldn't agree more. But I knew what I had to do, to put it right. I went to Temple and prayed for forgiveness. To which I am entitled. And which I didn't get."

"I explained about that," I said.

He didn't seem to have heard me. "And after that it was all consequences. All my land and property taken away, a jail cell, the noose, eternal damnation." He shook his head. "I could've accepted that," he said. "It was only fair. It was right and proper. And then you show up."

"Just as well for you that—"

"Be quiet. You showed up. With a snap of the fingers, you undo it all. I'm free, I'm pardoned, I get all my stuff back. In the eyes of the law, I didn't do anything bad at all. But that's *wrong*. You shouldn't be able to do that."

"All right. I won't bother."

He ignored me. "Instead," he said, "I get let off if I play a game for you. Entertainment. Something to help you pass the weary hours of eternity. And you can go around stopping hearts, sending plagues, burning down cities, anything you want, and there are no consequences whatsoever. Why? Why is it like that?"

I gave him the frostiest look I could manage. "I'm sure you're going to tell me."

"Because you're stronger. For the same reason Lysippus could make me eat worms when we were kids. Because he could hold me down with one hand and stuff worms in my mouth with the other, and no matter how hard I struggled, all my strength put together couldn't match his, and the more I fought, the more he laughed. Because he was stronger; no other reason."

I'm really rather proud of how well I kept my temper. "All right," I said. "Yes. Call it stronger if you like. The truth is, we're a higher form of life than you are, and therefore we're *entitled.* Our superiority gives you the right. Like you've got the right to kill pigs and chickens."

For some reason that made him smile. "Higher and superior," he said. "You honestly believe that."

"Of course."

"Mphm." He beamed at me. "Superior," he repeated.

"*Yes.* Like you're superior to your serfs and tenants, which means they have to work all day in the blazing sun while you loaf about. And what do you think would happen to you if you killed one of them? Let's just suppose that, for argument's sake. Suppose one of your servants was standing where you are now, and just for the hell of it you pushed him off the cliff. Well?"

He was quiet for a long time, and I was sure I'd beaten him. Then he said; "Until I met you, I'd have known what the consequences would be. I'd have known that I'd be punished for my crime with eternal damnation, because the gods are just and good, because that's what they're *for.* Now, though—"

He grinned at me, and I'm afraid something snapped. I have a temper, I admit it. I yelled something at him and suddenly there was this ferocious gust of wind—like I said earlier, bad things happen when we get angry—and it caught him up and swept him backwards over the edge of the cliff.

OH, I CAUGHT him, needless to say. I was there so fast, I'd have had time to comb my hair and do my nails. I cradled him in my strong arms, like a mother with her baby, and floated back up to the top.

"Don't say anything," I told him. "Don't say a word."

THE NEXT MAJOR obstacle was crossing the Great North Sea.

We stood on a shingle beach. The tide was coming in fast, frothy and the wave-crests white as milk. I'd conjured up a ship well in advance. It was riding at anchor fifty yards offshore, in a little cove.

"If it's all the same to you," I said, "I'll fly. Meet you on the other side."

He looked at me sideways. "I have no idea how you work these things."

"It's easy. Hoist the sail, then steer with the rudder. To make it stop, there's a big stone with a rope tied to it."

"You're going to fly."

"I get seasick."

Stupid lie, but it was all I could come up with in the heat—make that the freezing cold panic—of the moment. I have no issues whatsoever with the sea, of course. It's just water, with a pinch of salt.

"I could take the long way round," he said. "Follow the coast, dry land all the way. It adds three weeks to the trip, but there'd be no fooling around with boats."

"Don't be such a baby," I told him. "Tens of thousands of mortals, your inferiors in birth, breeding and intelligence, make their livings sailing ships on the sea. If they can do it, so can you."

"But you're flying."

I smiled at him. "Do you want to spend a night and two days cooped up in something that size with me?"

He thought about it, not for very long. "For the record," he said, "I think this is a terrible idea."

I watched him set sail, arranged a favourable wind, then turned myself into a seagull. I spread my wings and flew as high as I could. I was, of course, kidding myself. I hadn't gone far when a black speck swooped down at me right out of the sun. Before I had a chance to get out of the way, it grew into a huge grey-black cormorant; it crashed into me, closed its claws round my neck and plunged me down under the water. By the time I'd resumed my true shape, we were at the bottom of the sea, just outside the entrance to the Northern Palace.

"Hello, uncle," I said.

The cormorant changed instantly into my uncle Thaumastus. "I told you," he said. "Stay away from me."

"I was thirty thousand feet up," I protested.

"Thirty thousand feet over the sea. Therefore, on my turf. Where I told you never to come, ever again."

He wasn't a cormorant any more, but he was still gripping my neck. All gods are infinitely strong, but some gods are infinitely stronger than others. "Let go," I said. "You're hurting me."

He scowled at me. "That's you all over," he said. "You never will do as you're damn well told."

"I'm sorry." The words came out as a squeak. "I was blown off course."

"Like hell you were." He narrowed his eyes and peered at me, as though I were truly atrocious handwriting. "No, I know you, you're up to something."

"That's so unfair."

"You're always up to something. You're devious. I wouldn't believe you if you told me my name."

"That's a very hurtful thing to say, uncle."

He looked up, his fish-eye vision taking in the underside of every ship on the North Sea. "Which one is it?"

"I have no idea what you're talking about."

"You wouldn't dare come on my turf if you weren't protecting some mortal. So, I'll ask you again. Which one?"

"You're completely wrong. I was blown off course. It's the truth."

"Fine," he said. "I'll sink them all, then."

Damn, I thought. "You please yourself," I said. "Since none of them mean anything to me, why should I care?"

He grinned. "That proves it," he said. "If you weren't up to something, you'd be giving me a hatful of sanctimonious spiel about not killing mortals. I think it's the thing I dislike most about you, that awful self-righteous pomposity."

Overhead, I could hear the winds howling and the waves roaring. Damn and blast. "Is that it?" I said. "Can I go now?"

He glared at me. Yes, he's much stronger than me, but there's still nothing at all he can do to harm me. He could lock me up in his dungeons, but I'd make a real mess of the structural integrity of his palace when I broke out. "Piss off," he said. "And don't ever come back."

He let go; I transformed into a little silver fish, shot up through the water, broke the surface and changed into a goose. Geese are fast, with good eyesight. It was blowing a gale up there. Waves as tall as mountains towered, crashed and pounded all about me. I quickly calculated Lord Archias' likely course, making corrections in speed and bearing for the wind and waves; in a fraction of a second I'd got him pinpointed. I soared down and sure enough, bobbing about in the foam I saw the shattered timbers of a wrecked ship. For a moment I thought I might have come too late; but then a hand broke the surface, scrabbled for a grip on a length of shattered mainmast. I launched into a dive, turned myself into a giant osprey, gripped the hand in both talons and made a beeline for the shore.

"You knew," he said.

"Rubbish."

It had taken me a while to get all the water out of his lungs. When he spoke, his voice was low, quiet and rasping. "You knew something like that was going to happen. That's why you flew."

"I didn't know," I yelled. "It was just a precaution."

He blinked his bloodshot eyes. "Ah."

"My uncle the Sea King and I don't get on," I said. "If he'd seen me on a boat with you, he might have—well, played rough games. So, for your sake, to make sure you wouldn't be interfered with, I decided to make my own way."

"I sank."

"Coincidence."

"A storm came up out of a clear blue sky."

"It happens," I said. "It's something to do with cold fronts from the mountains colliding with water vapour rising from the seasonally warm Gulf Stream. Read a book about it, it's all in Saloninus' *Geography*."

"You made me sail in a boat," he said, "knowing your uncle would sink me on sight."

"I keep telling you, I didn't *know*. There was a risk, but definitely not a certainty."

He sighed. "It's true," he said, "what people say. Your whole life does flash in front of your eyes. I never believed it, but it's true."

"Oh come on," I said. "You were never in any real danger. You knew I'd save you."

"I was breathing in water." He stopped. I recognised the abrupt silence. It means *it's no good arguing with her, she doesn't listen*. I found that insulting. "So," he said. "What's the quarrel about?"

"What quarrel?"

"You and your uncle the Sea King. What did you do to him?"

"Nothing."

"Oh really. He sinks your favourites' ships on sight because of nothing."

"He's an idiot," I snapped. "And ridiculously oversensitive. And he bears grudges over the least little thing."

"Such as?"

"None of your business. Family stuff. Private."

He shrugged. "Suit yourself. It's not like I'm interested or anything."

"He's *impossible.*" It just came flooding out. Well, who have I got to talk to about anything, in the normal run of things? "He's got absolutely no sense of proportion."

"That," Lord Archias said gravely, "I can believe."

"It was years ago," I said, "and it all came to nothing anyway, and we weren't going to do anything *nasty* to him, and Zenonis would've made a much better Sea King. And it's a complete lie saying I was the ringleader, I barely knew a thing about it, most of the time I wasn't even there. It's so unfair."

He was gazing at me. "You conspired to overthrow the Sea King," he said. "And you can't understand why he's upset."

"Oh be quiet," I said. "You don't know anything about anything."

MORTALS ARE USELESS at most things, but they write good literature. I don't go much on the shorter stuff, because most of it's, well, a bit too mortal-specific for my taste, all about the human condition, and therefore not particularly interesting. But I like some of the plays. There's one about a great human hero—name's on the tip of my tongue—who offends one of the gods and is driven mad. In his madness, he kills his wife and his baby children. When he comes round out of it, his best friend tries to make him feel better. It wasn't your fault, says the friend, the gods made you do it. Don't you dare say such a thing, the hero replies. I believe in the gods, they're noble and good. They represent everything that is holy and perfect in the Universe, and I won't hear a word against them. All the stories the poets tell about how they sleep with their sisters and bind each other in chains are just blasphemous nonsense.

Well; quite right about the sleeping-with-sisters. I'm terribly fond of Pol, but I wouldn't touch him with a ten-foot pole, not in that way. The binding each other in chains, however, is rather more factually accurate. Adamant is the only material that seems to work, incidentally; iron's useless, naturally; over the years we've fooled around with beryllium, titanium, monomolecular polymers and various different carbon fibres, but no joy so far. Adamant, however, appears to get the job done, or at least it has so far.

Please don't think we make a habit of it, or do it lightly. Father had to tie up Grandpa when he took over, because Grandpa's got a filthy temper and it's just conceivably possible that he knows how to end the Universe. And we had to chain up the Giants, because of their persistent and incorrigible antisocial behaviour; and anyway, they're not real gods, just a bunch of invulnerable immortals with supernatural powers. My aunt Epicasta brought it on herself, and all she has to do is say she's sorry and she can come out again; it's just silly pride and spite that's kept her down there all these years. Like I say, it's a very rare occurrence.

And yes, on balance I think it was probably a mistake to try and overthrow uncle Thaumastus. It's perfectly true that he can be a complete beast at times—well, as witness his unreasonable behaviour in this case. But I have my suspicions that the motivation behind that particular conspiracy had less to do with uncle bringing the Godhead into disrepute and more to do with aunt Zenonis wanting his job. Why, I can't begin to imagine. I wouldn't do it if you paid me.

It goes without saying, it doesn't *mean* anything. Take Grandpa. I readily concede, he's flat on his face, with chains on his wrists and ankles and Mount Gargettus on the small of his back, so he can't move about much or read or anything, but he's not *injured* in any way. At some point in the future, it's more or less inevitable he'll get loose again, and then there'll be hell to pay, believe me. The Giants are cooped up in the Pit, but they're perfectly healthy, just bored out of their walnut-sized minds; same goes for aunt Epicasta. There's nothing permanent about any of it. For the gods, nothing is permanent, except existence. It goes without saying, no god has ever killed another. We couldn't, even if we wanted to. Therefore, anything we do to each other can never amount to more than a temporary nuisance. This is probably just as well.

So, I was quite right. Lord Archias couldn't possibly understand the nature of divine feuding. Incapable of understanding, he certainly shouldn't have presumed to pass judgement.

You can see why I was upset.

WE WENT THE long way round.

It's pretty boring traipsing all the way round the coast, but at least Lord Archias could catch fish to eat. I helped him a bit there; he must've realised, because after a while he stopped baiting the hook, but he didn't say anything. Mostly I sent him sturgeon, and the ones he didn't want he sold to passing locals, thereby making enough money to buy new shoes and clothes, flour and dried fruit, a hat, boring stuff that mortals are always concerned about. I just trudged along trying to occupy my mind. We didn't talk much. To be honest, I was pretty well fed up with the whole stupid enterprise. For two pins I'd have forgiven him or left him to do what he liked, only I didn't want the others sniggering at me. It's a standing joke in our family, I never finish anything I've started; it's not fair and I'm sick of it. So I stayed; plod, plod, plod across the horrible wet sand.

Then one day I happened to look out to sea and I saw twelve ships. I thought nothing of it—ships, yawn—but Archias noticed them and got terribly excited.

"You know who they are," he said. "They're the Hus."

I squinted into the sun. He was quite right. "So?"

"They're pirates."

"So?"

He stared at them, shading his eyes with the flat of his hand. "They must be heading for that village we passed this morning," he said.

"Quite possibly. It's all right, they won't see us."

"And there's a temple, and a monastery. I bet that's what they're after."

"I wouldn't be at all surprised. Come on, the tide's about to turn. I really don't want to get my feet wet."

"Don't you get it?" He looked at me angrily. "We've got to warn the village. The Hus are ruthless barbarians. They'll kill the men and sell the women and children into slavery."

I shrugged. "It's what they do. We haven't got time to interfere. Look, I wasn't going to tell you this, but the day after tomorrow it's going to slash down with rain over the Crabhook Pass. Therefore we need to be over the pass by tomorrow evening, or you're going to get soaked to the skin, catch a cold which turns into a fever, and be very ill. You don't want that, do you?"

He acted like he hadn't heard me. "The temple," he said, "happens to be one of yours. These savages are going to burn it to the ground, slaughter your nuns and piss on your smashed-up statue. Don't you care?"

I took a deep breath. Time for some straight talking. "No."

He couldn't have been more surprised if I've drenched him with ice-cold water. "What did you just—?"

"No," I said. "I don't care. I don't because I can't."

He sat down on the sand, as though his legs couldn't carry his weight any more. "I don't get it," he said.

I sat down next to him. "Listen," I said. "What can you hear?"

He frowned, concentrating like mad. "The lapping of the waves. Birdsong."

"Lucky you. I can hear prayers. Millions of them, all the damn time. For example; I can hear the nuns in the monastery chapel praying to me to protect them from the Hus—they know about them already, they've got a look-out. I can also hear the prayers of the Hus in their ships, invoking me in my aspect as Thurinn, goddess of plunder and the joy of battle. Lady Thurinn, they're praying, send us success and great riches, so that we can feed our starving children over the winter. Lady Thurinn, help us, for there is none other that fighteth for us, but only thou." I paused. "You see the problem."

He looked at me.

"The Hus aren't joking," I said. "For centuries they were peaceful shepherds, grazing their sheep and goats on the hillsides of their native fjords. But the sheep and the goats cropped the grass too close, the winds blew all the topsoil away, and now they go hungry. In desperation, about fifty years ago, they took to their ships and sailed into the terrifying realm of my uncle Thaumastus, in the wild hope of finding something out there to keep their families alive. After weeks of being hurled around by storms in open boats they made land-fall on the north coast of your stupid Empire. They were stunned at what they found. Here were people who had so much, when they had nothing at all. They prayed to me, naturally, and I suppose I must've given them the impression it was all right to take a few sheep and some rather crude and gaudy religious artefacts—they were my artefacts, and I didn't begrudge them. Ever since, not unreasonably, they've come back every year. Put yourself in my place. If they prayed to you, would you have the heart to refuse?"

He thought for a while. "In your shoes?"

"Yes."

"I'd have warned them about letting goats overcrop."

Smartarse. "Yes, well, I didn't. My aunt Agape covers agriculture. Faced with the fait accompli, what would you do? If you were in my shoes?"

"Miraculously cover their hillsides with topsoil and then warn them about the goats. To the gods, all things are possible, right? Only, I guess, some possible things are more time and trouble than others, so they don't get done."

I particularly dislike mortals with an answer to everything. "It's infinitely more complicated than that," I said. "If I interfered in something to do with agriculture, first I'd really piss off my aunt Agape, who isn't nearly as sweetly reasonable as me, second I'd probably screw up some big, extensive long-term strategy and ruin the ecology of half a continent." I gave him a moment to think about that, then went on, "To the gods all things are possible," I said, "but there's stuff we can do that we don't because it would make things worse, not better. Counterproductive, I think is the word I'm groping for."

"I see," he said. "In other words, you're very powerful but hopelessly badly organised."

EVENTUALLY WE REACHED the point we would've been at if my stupid uncle hadn't been so bloody-minded and Archias had crossed the sea by boat. I don't think Archias and I had said two words to each other for the past six days. He made a slight detour to a village, to sell sun-dried sturgeon and buy flour and stuff. I waited for him at the crossroads. He hadn't been gone long when a golden eagle swooped down out of the sky and perched on the finger-post.

I was mildly surprised. My uncle Gyges is usually a kestrel.

"What?" I said.

"You're in so much trouble."

I sighed. "Now what am I supposed to have done?"

"More what you haven't," uncle said. "You do know what date it is?"

"Not a clue."

He clicked his tongue. Eagles can't do that, but luckily nobody was watching. "Wilfully blind, more like."

"Fine. What's the stupid date?"

"Yesterday was the last day of the Greater Athanasia."

"But that's not till—" I froze. "What month is this?"

"Goosefeather."

Nuts. I'd lost track of time, plodding through the wilderness. The Greater Athanasia, held on the last three days of Deer Rut, is a huge and extremely important festival in my honour, held at the Great Theatre in Lyconessus. Every year I have to manifest myself as a thirty-foot pillar of fire on the last day. If I don't, apparently, there will be famine and plague, or the world will come to an end, or something like that. Anyway, an awful lot of mortals will get frightfully upset, probably start doomsday movements and religious wars, burn heretics, make a dreadful fuss generally. I'd never ever missed it, not once, ever.

"What happened?" I said. "Were there riots?"

Uncle shook his head. "No, everything went off just fine. One of the best festivals in years, they said."

"But I wasn't there."

"Ah." He pecked under his wing, then went on, "The priests have contingency plans laid on, just in case. Obviously they know you quite well. They've got twenty thousand gallons of rock oil in a giant cistern at the back of the Theatre, and a very ingenious syphon arrangement, works by hydraulic pressure or something like that. When it was clear you weren't going to show, they cranked it up, set light to it and hey presto, divine renewal for another year."

I was relieved, naturally, but also somewhat—oh, I don't know. Disappointed? Offended in some way? I couldn't say.

"Well then," I said. "No harm done."

"You're still in big trouble. He wants to see you, now. Quick sharp. If you won't come, I'm to drag you by your hair."

He was perfectly capable of doing that. "Can't. I'm busy."

My uncle Gyges doesn't like me very much. "I was hoping you were going to say that."

"Yes, but I really am genuinely busy. Dad knows all about it. He approves."

I said the last two words in the shape of a dormouse, around which the talons of a golden eagle suddenly closed inexorably. "At least let me leave a note for the human," I squeaked, but I don't suppose he heard me over the rushing of the wind.

DAD WAS SEATED on the Throne of the Sun; always a bad sign. From there, he can look out over every corner of the world, and beyond, to the stars. It gives him a sense of perspective, he says; it reminds him that he really is the epicentre of the universe, master of all he surveys, the single most important entity in existence. I perceive it as a big gold chair, tastelessly overdecorated with prancing lions and anatomically impossible cherubim.

"You've done it this time," he said.

"Come off it," I said. "I missed a festival. The priests covered for me. It's all right."

He shook his head slowly, his beard touching one shoulder, then the other. "Afraid not," he said. "Really and truly, pumpkin, you've gone and made a terrible mess of things."

He explained. The festival was not, as I and ninety-nine per cent of the humans attending it believed, a bit of a spectacle and a chance to let off steam. It genuinely was an act of renewal—of the fertility of the earth, the balance of the forces of nature, the covenant between gods and mortals. Yes, the priests had faked it for me, so nobody but them knew that disaster was just around the corner; war, famine, pestilence, death. But within seventy-two hours there'd be earthquakes and a tidal

wave. A week after that, a disease would start wiping out
livestock. Bitter rain would fall, poisoning the rivers and
killing the growing crops. The temperature would rise by
at least three degrees, and so would sea level. All these
disasters would cause panic among the mortals, who'd
start blaming each other, giving credence to weird and
savage religious cults; there'd be war, leading to floods of
refugees crowding into the cities of the plain; more war,
more famine, more pestilence and more death. All my
fault. All because I couldn't be bothered to show up.

"But that's stupid," I said. "And why the hell did
nobody tell me?"

"You didn't know?"

"Of course not, or else I'd have made damn sure I
was there."

He frowned. "How could you not know?"

"Maybe because nobody saw fit to tell me?"

"Well, we assumed—" He closed his eyes, and sighed.
"Wonderful. What is it about this family? Why doesn't
anybody talk to anybody else?"

He didn't need me to tell him that. "So," I said. "What
are you going to do about it?"

"Me?" He looked genuinely surprised. "Nothing."

"You're just going to sit there and let thousands of
humans die."

And I didn't need to ask. I knew the answer. It
would be yes. Yes, because there wasn't really anything
he could do. Theoretically, of course; theoretically, he
could restrain the winds, order Thaumastus to hold
back the sea, press down the earth's crust with his foot

to stop the fissures opening, reach out his hand and pluck the plague birds out of the sky and lock them in an adamantine cage, blow a mighty breath to scatter the poison clouds—he could do all that, because to the king of the gods all things are possible. But he didn't have to, because nobody and nothing can make him do anything, and it wasn't his fault. And, when it comes right down to it, why should he? After all, they're only mortals. Plenty more, in a couple of dozen generations' time, where they came from.

"Please?" I said.

I KNEW IT wouldn't be that easy.

To do him justice, he saw to all the urgent business first, the holding back and the ordering and the stamping and the plucking and the puffing. Only when he'd finished with all that and was sure everything was going to be all right did he turn to me and pull a very sad face.

"Sorry, Pumpkin," he said.

"Dad—"

"This is going to hurt me," he said, " a lot more than it hurts you."

I got as far as "In that case—". Then he grabbed me by the ankle, swung me round his head three times and hurled me from the ramparts of heaven.

IT TAKES THREE days to fall. I spent them reflecting on various aspects of ethical theory.

First, I reflected (my ankle hurt where he'd squashed it in his great paw; my ankle is divine substance, therefore in theory impervious to feeling, but it didn't seem to make any difference. Presumably he wanted it to hurt, so it did), let's start with the Givens. The prime Given is that Might is Right. Right is, by definition, the will of the strongest, just as among humans the law is by definition the king's will. Pretty uncontroversial stuff. Nobody in their right mind's going to argue with that.

Except, I found myself doing so; mostly to pass the time, because three days with nothing to do except fall is *boring*. Is what the strongest wants necessarily Right? Well, of course it is.

To understand that, consider the meaning of the word Right. Doesn't take long to figure out that it doesn't actually mean anything. It's not like black or left or serrated or strawberry-flavoured; it has no objective meaning. 'Right' is just a shorthand way of saying 'what we think is right'. Because the strongest must always prevail, therefore, their notion of what they think is right must also always prevail. Glad we'd got that settled.

And the alternative; simply doesn't bear thinking about. The alternative would require the existence of some absolute ideal of Right, supervening and more powerful than the strength of the strongest. Right would confront the strong over some contentious issue, and the strong would back down, tails between legs. Bullshit. Pure fantasy.

No, go back to the true definition of right; what we think is right. The key words are 'what we think'. Which is why I'd prevailed over my father, by using the magic word 'Please'. Short for, if it please you. If it pleases you to do what I ask, regardless of the fact that you don't have to and nobody can make you. Also implied; if it pleases you to do this thing and thereby win my gratitude and good opinion; because, for someone like you who can have any material thing he wants just by snapping his fingers, the only thing left that you might want and not be able to get just by commanding, is the gratitude and good opinion of others. Their love.

Objection, I objected. To the gods, all things are possible, and the strongest prevails even over the strong. If he were to *command* me to love him, I'd have no choice. But of course he'd know. He'd know I didn't really love him, it was just magic.

That, of course, is why he'd thrown me off the ramparts of heaven (this is going to hurt me more than it hurts you); and why I really didn't want to be thrown. Physical injury was out of the question. The true horror of the ultimate divine sanction isn't mere bodily discomfort. It's having all the others snigger at you behind their hands for the rest of eternity, the perpetual loss of face, which never goes away and never heals. Shame is the word I'm looking for here. Honour on the one hand, shame on the other. Right is what brings you honour, wrong is what brings you shame. Which is why we bother with mortals—all right, their good opinion isn't worth a lot, they're only mortals, but when you're poor, dirt-poor as the gods when it comes to things of real value (meaning things you want and can't have for the asking), even the good opinion of mortals counts for something. Like the love of a dog. It's only a dog, but it still counts for something.

The amusing thing is that mortals don't understand this. They believe in monolithic, abstract, objective Right and Wrong. Asked to define these terms, sooner or later they're forced to admit that Right is that which pleases the gods, Wrong is what pisses them off. Even the few mortals who don't believe in us think that way, except that in their case, right is defined as that which we were taught is pleasing to the gods, back when we believed in them—the ancient pie-in-the-sky confidence trick, whereby the stronger are kidded into subjugating themselves to the weaker, in consideration of goodies, trinkets and shiny beads once they're dead. Lord, what fools these mortals be.

So, I thought; why am I doing this? To gain the good opinion of one lousy mortal. What makes him special? He's met me, he's seen me in my true form, he's been granted the ultimate transcendental vision of the Deity, and he *doesn't like me*. This makes him special; make that unique (blessed are those who have seen and yet have not believed). Therefore, I am doing this to win the good opinion of one mortal, because it's precious to me; because I can't have it.

And then the ground jumped out at me and hit me.

IN YEARS TO come they'd call it the Great Asteroid Crater. I climbed out of it, dusted myself off and looked round to see where I was.

Believe it or not, even though I've been living on and around Earth for millennia beyond counting, there are still some places I've never been. This was one of them. It took me a moment to get my bearings, until I saw the unmistakable profile of the Sugarloaf Mountain far away on the western horizon. That put me about dead centre of the Sparkling Desert, on parts of which rain has never fallen, and where you can fry an egg on a rock. I was about to sprout wings and get the hell out of there when I happened to look down at my feet, and saw a nugget of gold the size of my thumb.

Oh dear, I thought.

It wasn't the only one. My impact crater had revealed a phenomenally rich seam of gold-bearing quartz; one which, in the normal course of events, would have stayed safely hidden for more or less ever. Now, though—it was only a matter of time before some wretched mortal stumbled across it; another matter of time, probably weeks, before the dreary, lethal desert all around me was covered with shacks, shanties and the headstones of fools. I quickly conjured a freak rainstorm, which turned the crater into a lake, but I knew I was kidding myself. In a few days' time the murderous heat of my uncle Actis would evaporate the water, leaving the deadly lure once more exposed. Unintended consequences, I thought. Hundreds, probably thousands of dead miners; billions of guldens' worth of unsupported specie, fuelling inflation, destabilising economies, collapsing markets and ruining lives. Not my fault; I had no control over where I'd landed. Just one of those things.

Or, if you happen to be a true believer; if a god falls to Earth, naturally you'd expect to find something rich and rare at ground zero. Everything the gods do, every trace they leave is wonderful and perfect; pure gold. It's the greed and folly of men that causes all the trouble.

THIS RELATIVITY-TIME-DISCREPANCY THING is a total bitch. As far as I was concerned, I'd only been away long enough to fly to heaven and fall back down from it; twenty minutes plus three days. In Lord Archias' timescale, however—

"I'm here to see the prisoner," I said.

The warder looked at me. "What, 5677341 Archias?"

I'd taken the precaution of dressing up as a drop-dead-gorgeous honey blonde, a type that seems to appeal to prison guards everywhere. "Yes, if that's all right."

"Why?"

"I'm his wife," I said sweetly.

Stunned silence, of a level of profundity I can't remember having experienced since the world was very, very young. "You're kidding. You, married to him?"

I nodded. "I've come to pay his fines and his debts and get him released."

The guard rolled his eyes. "This way," he said.

Archias was sitting on the floor—no comfy stone benches in provincial jails—staring down at his feet. He looked up when the door opened. His face creased as though with pain.

"Oh for God's sake," he said.

"Hello."

Mute anguish filled his eyes. "I thought," he said, "I honestly thought, after all this time, I'd finally got rid of you."

"Three days?"

He glowered at me. "You what? It's been six months. Six happy, happy—"

"How long have you been in here?"

"Five months."

"How long are you in for?"

"Twenty years. But I didn't mind. Really, I didn't mind one bit."

"What did you do?"

"Huh? Oh, I stole a loaf of bread, because I was penniless and starving. But so what, no big deal. I was free of you, that was all that mattered."

Twenty years in solitary for stealing a loaf. That's what right-and-wrong leads to. "Well," I said, "it's all right, I'll have you out of here in no time and then we can carry on with the quest. So that's all right."

Oh, the infinite weariness as he rose to his feet. "Don't be silly," I said. "You can't want to stay in here."

"Can't I?"

"Don't be such an ungrateful pig."

I left him and went to pay his fine—twenty years, for stealing a loaf, or a forty-kreuzer fine; justice. I found the governor. Paying was embarrassing, because the smallest coin I had on me was a one-gulden, and nobody had any change. They had to send a runner to the wine-shop. No, really, I protested, keep the change. The governor looked at me darkly; we aren't allowed to do that. Then spend it on the welfare of the prisoners. He didn't even bother to reply to that.

I GAVE HIM the sixty kreuzers; he bought new clothes and shoes, provisions, maps, a sword, lots and lots of rope. "Thank you," he said, rather grudgingly.

"You're welcome."

"I'll pay you back, naturally, if we ever get back home." I laughed. "Forget it," I said.

"No. I pay my debts. It's a point of honour."

I smiled at his choice of words. "I wouldn't bother," I said. "It's not like it was even real money. I just conjured a one-gulden piece out of thin air."

He froze. "You paid my fine with counterfeit money."

"Well, I suppose, technically—"

"You stupid—" He gazed at me. "You do realise, the penalty for passing false coin in these parts is death?"

"Don't make such a fuss," I said. "Anyway, they'll never be able to tell the difference."

He wasn't listening. He was looking back over his shoulder. Out of the city gate rode a squad of troopers in shiny armour. They kicked up a big cloud of dust, and they were heading straight at us. He looked at me.

"Run," he said.

WE SPENT THE next three nights cowering in ditches. "We can't explain," he told me, "or talk our way out of it. Passing false coin is what they call an offence of strict liability. If they can prove you were in possession of a counterfeit coin, you swing. That's it."

"Really?" I was shocked. "That's not justice."

He shrugged. "It's the law. And you can see their point. Counterfeit money wrecks economies."

"But we didn't do anything wrong. Well, you didn't."

"Doesn't matter. Makes no odds. Strict liability."

"And you *approve* of that?"

He shrugged. "I believe in the rule of law," he said.

Presumably he also believed that the gods don't bind each other in chains. Humans, eh?

THE JURISDICTION OF the loathsome little settlement where we'd committed our dreadful crime ended on the edge of the White Desert. Once we'd set foot on the sand, we were safe.

He looked out over the endless dunes. "How far—?"

"A hundred and seventy-two miles."

When he'd gone shopping, he'd bought four quart water-canteens, guaranteed leak and evaporation proof. Unfortunately, what with all the running away we'd been doing, we'd neglected to fill them with water.

"Don't worry about it," I said. "You've got me with you, remember?"

He solemnly unslung the canteens from around his neck and threw them away, one by one. "Of course." he said. "Silly me."

"Last stage of the journey," I said encouragingly. "We'll be there before you know it."

A change came over Lord Archias when we were in the White Desert. He stopped whining and complaining about every last little thing. In particular, he stopped being so very difficult about accepting help. When he was thirsty, he let me materialise silver jugs of iced water, which he gulped down and thanked me for. Encouraged by this, when we stopped for the evening I conjured up a nice comfy tent, with silk cushions and a dinner table loaded down with his favourite dishes. It gets very cold in the desert at night, so I cast a warming aura round the tent, and he didn't bat an eyelid. Of course, I couldn't resist asking him why the change in attitude.

"I've given up," he replied, and helped himself to more cold roast lamb.

"Given up," I said. "What's that supposed to mean?"

He swallowed his mouthful and washed it down with iced jasmine tea. "It means," he said, "that suddenly you are my shepherd, wherefore shall I lack nothing. You make me lie down in green pastures. Why, I can no longer be bothered to speculate. Any minute now I expect you'll change your mind or simply forget all about me and go swanning off again, and then I'll die of heat-stroke. So, why not enjoy what's going while I can?"

I was shocked. "What sort of an attitude is that?"

"I think it's called pragmatism," he said with his mouth full. "If you mean, why have I stopped fighting for what I believe in and sold out to a corrupt and decadent theocratic regime—" He did a huge shrug. "We're in a desert," he said, "with no camels and no water. So I've got two choices, sell out or die. I've always taken the view that staying alive is a useful prevarication, keeping all options open. And you can't drink pride."

"You're just full of it," I said.

"Pride?"

"No."

The journey across the desert was actually rather nice, if you like warm sunshine. Once we got past the dunes it was all very flat, so none of that wretched walking uphill (I was back in a physical body, to catch some rays). I never could see the point of gradients. If I had to be a mortal for any length of time, *down with up* would be my battle-cry. Lord Archias was mercifully quiet, practicing his newly-minted philosophy of unquestioning acceptance. I must confess I spoiled him rather, plenty of nice food and cold drinks and soft cushions to sleep on. He actually put on a bit of weight—he'd got terribly skinny while I was away—and by the time we reached the Something-or-Other oasis which marked the halfway mark, he was in pretty good condition, bright eyes and glossy hair. A bit dispirited, maybe, but that was better than having him yapping all the time.

I had to spoil it by opening my big mouth. "I'm really glad," I said, as we sat under the shade of a tree at the edge of the oasis, "that you've finally realised that I've got your best interests at heart."

"Mphm."

I offered him a box of dried figs, dusted with icing sugar. He took one. "I have, you know," I said. "I want you to succeed on this mission, and get your life back, and be happy. And I want you to have gained by the experience, to have learned something from it."

"Oh, I've done that all right."

"Good."

He yawned and helped himself to another fig. "Years ago," he said, "I remember talking to a merchant who'd come to sell my father something or other, and he told me that he'd once been to a faraway land and met someone who told him stories from his religion."

"In the faraway land?"

"That's right, yes. Apparently they've never heard of you over there."

I frowned. "Really?"

"It's a very, very long way away, this merchant told me. He said that out there, they only really believe in the Skyfather, or the Invincible Sun, I forget which. Anyhow, just the one god. Your father, presumably."

"Ignorance is a terrible thing."

"It must be, yes. Anyway, there was one story I really liked. In the story, the Skyfather or the Invincible Sun or whatever he's called holds a party in heaven for all his angels and thrones and cherubim, and one of the guests is the angel in charge of temptation."

I yawned. "I don't think I've heard this one. Go on."

"Anyway, the tempter gets talking with Skyfather, and he asks him; do the mortals love and respect you, like they should? Of course, Skyfather says. Fine, says the tempter, so long as you pamper them and give them treats. But suppose you stopped doing that. Suppose you started smiting them instead. I bet you they'd stop loving and respecting you like a shot. I don't think so, Skyfather said. Really, said the tempter, in that sniffy sort of a way. Really, said Skyfather, and I'll prove it to you. So he chose his most devoted and faithful worshipper, a man he'd showered with presents and made very rich and contented; and all in one day he took away all his wealth, stripped him of his honours and titles and left him penniless. See, Skyfather said to the tempter, he still believes in me, he still loves and respects me. All right, said the tempter, now let's see how he'll react if you really make him suffer. So Skyfather robbed him of his wife and his best friend, and had him thrown into a stinking dungeon. And the man—the merchant did tell me his name but I've forgotten—the man started moaning and complaining, my god, my god, why hast thou forsaken me? What did I ever do wrong? Why are you doing this to me? And when Skyfather couldn't stand his whining any longer, he appeared to him and said, where were you when I laid the foundations of the earth? What do you know about anything? You have no idea why I do what I do, so quit griping and adore me. Which the man did; whereupon Skyfather let him out of jail and gave him his money and his titles back, and the official version is that he lived happily ever after. And he never did find out that Skyfather had done all these horrible, cruel things to him because the tempter had made a complete fool out of Skyfather and twisted him round his little finger." He paused, then added, "At least, I think that's how the story went. I may have got some of the details wrong."

I frowned. "It couldn't have been my father," I said. "He's way too sharp to be taken in like that."

"Ah. That's all right, then."

"It just goes to show," I said. "If people will insist on worshipping weak, gullible gods, they get what they deserve. You're far better off with our lot. We haven't got a tempter."

"Really."

"Don't need one," I said proudly.

IN THE PRISON cell, before we started the journey, I'd promised to draw Archias a map. I always keep my word.

"This," I said, pointing, "is the Portals of the Sunset, and here's the River of Lost Souls and the Bridge of Forgetfulness. And my aunt's place is right here."

He looked up at me. "You're leaving me?"

"Just for a bit. I have some things I need to see to. But it's perfectly all right, I've left a trail of water-jugs and hampers of food that'll lead you right there. Just carry straight on, you can't miss it."

"All right."

"Now," I said, "there's some stuff you'll need; a lamb, and a sharp knife, and a bowl, and two gold coins. I've arranged for someone to meet you at the Bridge and give them to you."

"Thank you."

"Now then, look after yourself while I'm gone. Be careful."

"I don't need to look after myself," he said. "I've got you."

Just occasionally, mortals can be so sweet. "That's right, you have."

"I've decided that from now on I'm going to trust my elders and betters," he said. "It was thinking about that merchant that made my mind up for me—you remember, the one who'd been to the faraway land? He had another story." He smiled. "Sorry, I don't want to hold you up. I'll tell you when you get back."

"I've got plenty of time," I said. "Tell me the story."

"Oh, all right then." He folded the map I'd drawn him and tucked it neatly into the lining of his hat, where it'd be safe. "The merchant told me that in another faraway land, a different one, there lived a great and mighty people. As they grew and prospered, they needed more land for houses and farms. Now in the west of their country there was plenty of good land, but a few savages lived there, sleeping in felt tents and hunting for food with stone arrowheads. So the great and mighty people went out to build houses and stake out farms in the west, and the savages tried to stop them, shooting at them with their flint arrows. The great and mighty people could have killed all the savages very easily, but instead they said to them, Give us your land, and in return we'll let you have a very small part of it to live in, and we'll give you food to eat and strong liquor to drink, and in time you can learn to be just like us. So that's what the savages did, and there they still are, what's left of them, to this day. They trusted the goodness and compassion of the strong, and it all came out right for them in the end."

"There you are, then," I said.

I HADN'T BEEN entirely honest with Lord Archias. I didn't slip away because I had business of my own to see to. Instead, I turned into a falcon and flew over the desert to my aunt Feralia's house.

I suppose Feralia is my favourite aunt, which in real terms means the one who dislikes me least. I think that has a lot to do with the fact that we almost never see each other. But she knows that I'd be prepared to go and see her, if it wasn't for the fact that she lives in the perpetual darkness and unbearable cold of the Kingdom of the Dead.

Her house has no windows and no doors. The only way in or out is through the walls, thirteen feet thick, solid rock. If you can't walk through walls, you have no business arriving or leaving there. Inside (as I perceive it) there's just the one unthinkably vast big room, where Auntie sits on her black throne, with the souls of the dead cowering at her feet. She just sits there, doesn't even knit or read a book. Wouldn't suit me. I get bored very easily.

She looked up and saw me. "I'm very busy," she said. "Can't you come back later?"

Just kidding, of course. "Hello," I said. "I've got a favour to ask."

"What?" She scowled at me. "If he's thrown you out and you're looking for somewhere to stay, you can forget it. I haven't got the space."

Down at floor level, the spirits of the dead sniggered and chittered. "No," I said, "it's not that. I'd like to borrow something."

"What?"

I looked around until I found the ghost of the musician Lysippus. I pointed. "That."

There was a long silence. "What do you mean, borrow?"

"Well, you know. Take it away with me, for a bit. I'll bring it back when I've finished with it, I promise."

"Don't be stupid," she said. "You know that isn't possible."

"To the gods—"

"Oh, don't give me all that rubbish. You know your father would skin me alive."

I gave her my winning smile. "Suppose I brought a mortal here," I said, "and he challenged you to a game of, oh I don't know, chess or something, and if he wins you let me borrow Lysippus, and if you win, the mortal stays here for ever. That'd be all right, surely."

"No."

I pouted. "It's only borrowing," I said, "I'm not asking you to *give* me anything. It'd be like parole. You'd have him back again in no time. You wouldn't even notice he'd been gone."

"I'd notice."

I came a little closer and lowered my voice. "Dad wouldn't have to know about it."

"Your father has already given permission for this idiotic stunt, as you well know. It doesn't make the slightest bit of difference. The dead do not return."

"How would it be," I said, "if I borrowed Lysippus and I gave you Lord Archias, to keep, for your very own? A life for a life. That way, the equilibrium of life and death would be preserved."

"What equilibrium? You're talking nonsense. I'm not running a business here, I don't need to balance the books. Now go away, you're unsettling the stock."

She had a point. The spirits of the dead were getting restless, quivering and shivering and yapping. I knew why, of course. I was still in a physical form, and my body heat had raised the temperature by some infinitesimally tiny fraction of a degree, and now they were all too hot. And she couldn't open a window, because there weren't any.

"Please," I said.

But she shook her head. "Doesn't work on me," she said. Then she grinned. "I wouldn't have thought it possible, but you're even more stupid than you look. You made a ridiculous bargain with your father about getting Lysippus back from the dead, and you've come all this way, and you haven't actually got a plan. Well, have you? You probably thought, it's all right, I'll think of something when I get there. And you haven't. Have you?"

"There's no need to be grumpy," I said.

"To the gods all things are possible, you told yourself, of course you'd think of something. But not in this case, because there's nothing to think of. You can't have him. That's final." She sighed, then something like a smile spread over her regrettably featureless face. "You did your best," she said. "I'm sure you'll be able to talk your father round. You always were his favourite."

News to me. "Really?"

"Of course, didn't you know? Daddy's little girl. So don't worry, it'll all sort itself out, you'll see." The smile broadened a little. "Now, since you're here, let me get you something to eat. You must be famished after your long journey."

I backed away. "Thanks awfully," I said. "But—"

"Oh, go on. I insist. A nice cup of tea and maybe a few pomegranate seeds. Just a little snack to keep you going."

I'd been wondering why she'd suddenly started being nice. "No, really," I said. I backed away until I could feel the wall against my heel. "And besides," I added, as I slid into the masonry, "you said yourself, you haven't got the space."

SHE WAS WRONG, of course. I had thought of something before I went in. I'd thought of the subtle difference between having and borrowing. Pity it hadn't worked.

Ah well. Plan B.

I SAT ON a mountaintop somewhere and watched Lord Archias walking the last hundred miles. He took his time, which was sensible, drank plenty of water and always wore his hat. I could see his lips moving, which puzzled me, so I listened closely. He was actually praying as he walked—to me, mostly, but also to Dad, Pol, uncle Actis and aunt Cytheria—and when he wasn't praying he was singing hymns and arias from sacred cantatas. He was completely alone, there wasn't another human being in a hundred and twenty miles, so obviously he wasn't doing it for show, since there was no-one to see him.

I was so engrossed in eavesdropping that I didn't notice Pol swooping down beside me; first I knew of it was when I heard his voice, saying, "What on earth does the clown think he's doing?"

"That's genuine faith," I said. "I converted him."

"He's up to something."

"I'm glad you've turned up," I said. "I'm going to need you after all."

"Oh." He didn't sound happy. "I've been thinking about that."

"Pol. Don't you dare back out now."

"It's just—" There was genuine anguish in his voice. "Have I got to? There must be another way."

"I tried it. Didn't work."

"Dad is going to be so angry."

"He's given his permission, remember?"

"I don't think you were entirely straight with him. Maybe he doesn't quite realise what you've got in mind."

I didn't comment on that. "It'll be fine," I told him. "I promise."

"Only—" He paused, took a deep breath. "You do realise they're all laughing at you."

Well, I can't say I was surprised. Thrown down from the ramparts of heaven; the ultimate degradation. The odd thing was, I didn't really feel it. True, I hadn't yet confronted a gathering of my family *en masse*. Still; I'd expected to be engulfed in a deluge of shame and self-depreciation, and I hadn't been. Somehow, without consciously debating the issue with myself, I'd arrived at the conclusion that if the episode reflected badly on anyone, it was on Dad, for over-reacting. And not even that. Just a bloody stupid system, that was all. Any cosmos that falls to bits if a goddess doesn't show up on time at a particular place is clearly shoddily engineered and unfit for purpose. Not my fault; so why should I feel bad about it?

"Let them," I heard myself say.

I think Pol was slightly stunned by that. "No big deal?"

"No big deal. It'd be different if I valued their opinion of me, but since I don't, who gives a shit?"

Somewhere in the distance, thunder rumbled. "You're going to get all sorts of stick," Pol said with a shudder. "They're already making up nicknames for you."

"Good for them. I'm not bothered."

"You can't really mean that."

"No, I'm serious," I said, suddenly realising that I was. "I got thrown off the ramparts, so what? It's the worst punishment; it's also the only punishment. So, sooner or later, it's going to happen to all of us. And when we've all taken the long drop, it's not going to matter any more. We won't snigger at each other, because we'll have been there too." I paused. "You know what that means?"

Pol thought for a moment. "Anarchy? Chaos?"

"Freedom," I said. "We'll be free."

Pol sniffed. "Same thing."

"Maybe. But just think. Dad won't be able to boss us around any more. We can do exactly as we like. To the gods, all things really will be possible. Well? Doesn't that thought excite you?"

"With my god of wisdom hat on? No, not really."

"Don't be so miserable. *Free*, Pol. No constraints whatsoever. That's—"

"Inaccurate," he said. "Actually, if you're right, and I sincerely hope you aren't, I anticipate seeing a lot more restraints around the place in future. Adamantine ones, probably. Not to mention a lot of mountains getting moved around, and a whole lot less freedom. Be careful what you wish for, Sis."

"Killjoy."

"Yes."

I shook my head, as though he was something annoying caught in my hair. "Be that as it may," I said. "You've got a job to do and I expect you to do it. All right?"

He sighed. "Fine," he said. "I'll be there."

"Promise?"

"Word of honour."

HOW TIME FLIES. I'd forgotten about that. I raced back to the White Desert, to find Lord Archias at the foot of the bridge. He'd built himself a little hut out of thorn bushes, with a corral out back for a small herd of goats. He'd also grown a beard. There were grey streaks in it.

"You're back, then," he said.

"Sorry, I got held up."

"No, that's fine." He was resting on the handle of a crude, wooden-bladed shovel. "I've just been planting the spring beans. Should be a much better crop this year, I've been digging in plenty of manure."

There was something different about him. "You seem quite happy here," I said.

He nodded. "I am," he said. "I've got everything I want. Fresh water, food, shelter, a shrine to the gods. What more could any man ask?"

"A bit lonely, though."

"And solitude, of course. The five pillars of happiness."

I clicked my tongue. "Well, I'm here now. We'd better get on with it."

He gave me a wistful look. "Do we have to go right now?"

"Yes. No time like the present."

"Mphm. Sorry, it's just that it's been so long, it's hard to recapture the sense of urgency, if you see what I mean." He laid his shovel down on the ground, looked over his shoulder at the goat-pen. "All right, which way?"

"Straight on over the bridge. I'll be right behind you. Don't look at me like that," I added. "I do mean right behind you. I've just got to get some things. I'll catch you up."

He sighed.

THUS IT WAS that, not very long afterwards, we walked up the long drive of my aunt Feralia's house. I carried a silver chalice. Lord Archias led two lambs on string halters.

"There doesn't seem to be a door."

"There isn't." I knocked on the wall three times. "Keep your mouth shut," I told him. "Don't say anything."

"Mphm. Look, do you actually need me here for anything? Because if not, I can wait outside."

"Quiet," I told him, then grabbed him by the wrist and led him through the wall.

Nothing, it goes without saying, had changed since I was there last. Auntie didn't appear to have moved so much as an inch on her throne. Around her feet the squeaking dead still clustered, like dogs begging at table. "Hello, auntie, it's me again."

"You're back. Why?"

"I've brought Lord Archias with me," I said brightly. "If it's all right, he'd like to have a quick word with Lysippus."

"Would he really."

"Yes. He wants to apologise. Don't you?"

Archias was standing rooted to the spot, eyes bulging, mouth open. I gave him a warning tug on the wrist. "Don't you?"

"What? Oh yes. Please," he added, quite unprompted by me. Of course, it doesn't carry quite so much weight coming from a mortal.

Auntie looked at him, then back at me, trying to make up her mind. There is, of course, a protocol for such situations. Why there should be one or how it came to be formulated I have no idea. Mortals can't get into Auntie's house, because there is no door. In spite of that, there's a protocol.

It goes like this. If a mortal wants to ask a question of the dead, he must go to the House of the Dead (see above). Having received permission from the Queen of Death, he must then sacrifice a lamb and fill a silver chalice with its blood—that's all to do with the ancient superstition that blood somehow encapsulates the life-force; it does no such thing, but never mind. He pours a libation of blood onto the ground; the ghost he wants to question drinks the blood and is temporarily re-animated, resuming a simulacrum of his physical body for just long enough to answer the question. There's a bunch of other rules and regulations—no eating or drinking while you're there, no looking back over your shoulder as you leave, stuff like that—but basically that's it. Perfectly straightforward, if a bit archaic and pointless.

I realised I'd forgotten something. "Did you bring a knife?" I hissed in his ear.

He fumbled in his pocket and pulled out a flake of knapped flint. "Will this do?"

Not ideal; but I couldn't very well ask for the loan of one. No metal in Auntie's house, she's old-fashioned.

"That's fine," I said. "Kill the lamb and drain its blood into the chalice."

"Have I got to?"

"Kill the bloody lamb."

He did so, prising its head up with his crooked elbow under its chin to expose the throat. It struggled a few times, then relaxed and stretched out. The flow of blood into the cup sounded like an old man peeing.

"Permission granted." Auntie sat up just a little and sniffed a couple of times. "Who did you say he wants to talk to?"

"Lysippus, auntie. Lysippus son of—" I dried.

"Melias."

"Lysippus son of Melias of the deme of Mesogaea," I said. "Him," I added, and pointed.

Auntie nodded stiffly. I picked the chalice up off the floor and tilted it until a single drop of blood trickled over the rim and dropped (like a goddess falling from the ramparts of heaven) onto the dusty, quite filthy floor. The black splodge it made in the dust started to smoke. The smoke wavered and thickened, and became a man. Just a shape at first; then it sort of came into focus—eyes and a nose, then particular eyes and a particular nose, in a unique configuration that made an individual, rather than merely a generic human. He opened his eyes, blinked. "Archias?"

"Hello, Lysippus."

"Good God, man, I barely recognised you."

"It's been a while."

"Has it?" Lysippus frowned, as if trying to work out some impossible problem. "Didn't you just kill me?"

"Yes."

The look on Lysippus' face was that first-thing-in-the-morning, not-properly-awake stare. "You stabbed me."

"Yes."

"Why?"

"I caught you in bed with my wife."

"What? Oh, yes, so you did." Lysippus massaged his forehead with his fingers. "Look, I'm sorry about that."

"Forget it. These things happen. I shouldn't have killed you."

"No, maybe not." Lysippus closed his eyes, rubbed them with his thumbs, opened them again. "Still, I asked for it, didn't I? Come to think of it, I was always—well, doing stuff to you. All your life." He thought for a moment, then added, "I didn't think you minded."

"I minded."

"Yes, well, you would, wouldn't you? That's only reasonable. Strange I never appreciated it at the time." He frowned again. "I knew you hated it, actually, but deep down, I had this stupid notion, it was all just a game and it didn't mean anything. I guess I was wrong about that."

Archias nodded. "But I overreacted," he said. "I shouldn't have killed you."

"Well." Lysippus shrugged. "Makes no odds really, in the long run. I mean, nothing does, does it? You end up here, no matter what you do. Maybe a year or two earlier, but so what?"

I cleared my throat. "Does that mean you forgive him?"

For a moment neither of them seemed to know which one I was talking to. Then Lysippus said, "Sure, no hard feelings. Actually, it's not bad here. Peaceful. One day is very much like another, if you see what I mean."

He was starting to get faint. I let another drop fall to the floor. Some other ghosts tried to edge close, but I nudged them away with my foot. "It's important," I said, "that you forgive him. That you both forgive each other."

"Is it?" Lysippus looked at me blankly. "I forgive him. No problem."

"Archias?"

"What? Oh, me too."

There was a moment of awkward silence. The ghosts had stopped whinnetting; they were all gazing fixedly at the chalice. There was a whole lambful of blood in there, they seemed to be telling me, and I'd only used two drops. Shame to let the rest go to waste.

"There now," I said. "That wasn't too hard, was it?"

"Have you nearly finished?" aunt Feralia said. "Only, I hate to rush you, but I'm really very busy."

Archias gave me a despairing look. I shrugged. "Auntie," I said. "I know I asked before and you said no, but would you please, *please* lend me Lysippus son of Melias just for a few years, it'd make such a difference to me, I promise I'll bring him back in tip-top condition, as a special favour to me and I'll be utterly, utterly grateful and your slave for ever? Please, auntie? Please?"

"No."

"I think you're being really mean."

"I don't care."

"I think," I said, "that it's praiseworthy and honourable to do your job well and uphold the rules, but sometimes it's even more praiseworthy and honourable to bend the rules just a bit to help out a loved one or a family member in dire need, to the point where doing your job and upholding the rules to an unreasonable extent can actually be blameworthy and dishonourable, because you're putting your own honour above someone else's. That's selfish, which is dishonourable *per se*. It's also a tacit admission of weakness, because it's implying that the rules are stronger than you are, whereas a really strong person only obeys the rules when he wants to, because he agrees with them. I know that when you took this job you gave your solemn oath to see to it that the dead shall not return, but I think putting the rules and the rule of law above everything else is the sort of behaviour I'd expect from a mortal, because they're weak and they don't know any better. We should make it clear that to us all things are possible, including breaking our own word where necessary. I think that if you won't let me borrow Lysippus son of Melias, people will say it's because you're afraid of Father and being cast down from the ramparts of heaven, which I know isn't true because you're not afraid of anybody and anything, are you? Well?"

"You know what? I don't give a damn what you think."

Complete silence; even the ghosts had stopped twittering. Then Archias said, "That was your cunning plan? Sweet reason?"

"Be quiet," I told him. "Obviously we're wasting our time here. Sorry, but because of a certain person's intransigence, you can't have your forgiveness and I've been made to look a fool, and this whole quest has been for nothing. Well, auntie, it's your choice, if there are unpleasant consequences for you then on your head be it, I refuse to bear any responsibility. Come on, Archias, we're leaving."

I turned round, tugging him along behind me, straight through the wall and out into the fresh air.

"So that's it," he said.

"Yes."

He sat down on the last step of the bridge and buried his face in his hands. "You failed."

"Excuse me?"

"You failed."

I glared at him. "Can I just remind you," I said, "this was meant to be your quest and your assignment, and I was just along to give you help and moral support? If anyone's failed, it was you."

He looked up at me. "Bullshit," he said. "You've been in charge ever since we left the City, telling me what to do."

"You chose to take my help and advice. Your choice. Free will."

"*Bullshit.* I trusted you. Even when you weren't there, because you'd gone swanning off and forgotten me, I prayed to you. *You* were in charge, *you* decided what we were going to do, *you* failed."

I smiled at him. "Who says?"

He looked at me blankly. "What?"

"Who says I failed?"

"Don't be stupid. We went to get Lysippus. We left without him. Therefore—"

"Whatever became," I interrupted him, "of the second lamb?"

He opened his mouth, closed it again and looked round. "I guess I must've left it there. What possible difference—?"

"Hold still."

I leant forward. From the top of his boot, I pulled something like a flat, folded piece of parchment. I unfolded it. First I unfolded the small flat square into a full-size flat human silhouette. Then I unfolded the two-dimensional shape into three dimensions. A quick flick of tepid blood from the chalice brought it to life. "Behold," I said. "Lysippus son of Melias, in the flesh. I do *not* fail. Got that?"

I let go of Lysippus and he stumbled, then caught his balance and stood up. He saw Archias. "You," he said.

"Lysippus?"

"*Bastard!*" Lysippus roared, and hit Archias in the mouth so hard he fell over. "You killed me!" he roared, drawing his foot back for a kick. "You were my friend, and you damn well killed me!"

I caught hold of his hair and dragged him to his knees. "Yes, well," I said, "you're better now, so no harm done. And Archias came all the way here, at great trouble and expense, to bring you back to life. Say thank you."

I tightened my grip on his hair. "Thanks," he muttered.

"Sorry, I can't quite hear you."

"Thank you," he shouted. I let him go and he fell forward on his face. "Now then," I said. "I want you two to shake hands and be friends."

Archias spat out a tooth, then reached out his hand. Lysippus hesitated for a moment. I let my shadow fall across him. He grabbed Archias' hand, held it for a fraction of a second, then let go as though it was burning him.

"There," I said, "that's better. Everybody's friends with everybody else." I let Lysippus back off a pace or two, then I asked him, "What's the last thing you remember?"

"Him stabbing me, of course."

"Mphm. Would you like to go home now?"

"Yes." He stopped, then stared at me. "Goddess?"

"That's right."

He dropped to his knees and banged his forehead on the ground. "Forgive me. I meant no disrespect."

"Of course you didn't, that's fine. Now, are you friends with Archias again?"

"Yes, goddess. I love him like a brother."

"Splendid. Now, I'm going to send you home by magic. When you get there, you'll forget you ever saw me. You'll forget Archias ever hurt you. You'll live the rest of your life happily writing music and studying philosophy."

"Yes, goddess."

"Off you go, then." I snapped my fingers and he vanished.

Archias was looking at me. "Is he for real?"

"Excuse me?"

"Was that actually him? Or just one of your sockpuppets?"

I scowled at him for that. "That was the real, one and only Lysippus, son of Melias, of the deme of Mesogaea," I said. "He was dead but now he's alive again. I didn't fail. And you succeeded." I smiled. "You'll be a hero now," I said. "The stuff of legend. They'll write epics about you. Your name will never die. Won't that be nice?"

"But—"

I grinned at him. "The second lamb."

"What?"

I sat down beside him on the step. "You remember the second lamb."

"Yes."

"That," I told him, "was no lamb. That was my brother Polyneices, god among other things of shapes and illusions. While I was making my big, futile, impassioned speech and everybody was looking at me, Pol stopped being a lamb and turned back into himself, only invisible. He grabbed Lysippus' ghost, folded it up really small and stuffed it down inside your boot. Then he turned himself into the spitting image of Lysippus' ghost, while we made a quick getaway. Piece of cake," I added. "The old distraction routine. It never fails."

"Then your brother—"

"Is still in there, yes. But don't worry, he'll be fine, unless he eats or drinks anything, and he's too smart to do that."

"But the Lady of Death—Won't she be angry when she finds out?"

"Livid," I said. "Spitting feathers. But screw her. She was mean and she wouldn't help me when I asked her nicely, so nobody's going to have the slightest bit of sympathy. And Pol will just walk out through the wall and go home." I paused, expecting a torrent of praise. It didn't come. "Well?"

"You cheated."

"What? Well of course I cheated."

"It was a trick," he said bitterly. "It was a stupid trick. It was meaningless. It was *stealing*."

I shook my head. "Theft is taking with intent to permanently deprive the owner," I said. "In sixty years, she'll get him back again. Not theft, just borrowing."

"It's *childish*."

I realised I wasn't angry with him, in spite of his ingratitude. "I suppose it was, rather. But we're all a bit childish in my family. I guess childhood's the closest you mortals get to being us, when you're still too young to appreciate the implications of your own mortality." I smiled at him. "It's a shame you have to grow up, really."

He stood up. "I'd like to go home now, please. If you've finished with me."

"Of course. Close your eyes and you'll be there in two seconds."

"No," he said, "I didn't mean back to the City. I want to go *home*. There."

He was pointing at his stupid little hut, with the goat-pen out back. "You aren't serious."

"That's my home," he said. "I built it with my own two hands, and it rests on the five pillars of happiness. Four pillars," he amended. "I'm never going back. That's all right, isn't it?"

"Suit yourself," I said. "Oh, and you're forgiven."

"Am I? That's nice."

"That means," I said, slightly nettled, "that you won't suffer eternal damnation."

"No," he said. "Instead I'll end up in there, with her." He jerked his thumb back over the bridge. "Big difference."

"Aren't you at least going to thank me?"

"Thank you," he said. "Goodbye."

ON MY WAY home, I noticed a huge crater, just north of Perimadeia. I flew closer, and saw a small, sad-looking figure slowly climbing over the rim.

"Hello, Pol."

"Oh. It's you."

"Dad was cross, then."

"Yes. Dad was very cross."

"Sorry about that."

"It doesn't matter." He stopped and looked back over his shoulder. "Actually," he said, "you were quite right. I don't feel particularly bad about it. In fact, I couldn't really give a shit."

"Mphm. What about when all the others laugh at you and call you names?"

"Like I care. And besides, they won't. They'll be thinking, the old fool's losing it, it'll be my turn next." He looked at me. "The twilight of the gods, sis."

"Oh well."

"It's a pity, though. With honour and shame, we were just about viable. Without them—"

"No great loss."

"True. And to be honest with you, I'm so bored I don't much care. It's no fun being god of wisdom when you're a member of a race of idiots."

"In the kingdom of the stupid, the half-witted man is king."

He frowned. "Thank you," he said. "I think. It's the humans I feel sorry for. Without us, all they'll have is Right and Wrong. They'll get themselves in the most awful tangle."

"Still," I said, "there it is. Our time is up. When you gotterdammerung, you gotterdammerung."

He gave me a pained look. "That's truly awful," he said.

"Yes, well. I'm the goddess of laughter, all right?"

I don't think the pain on his face was just for the crummy joke. "Not for much longer, Sis."

You may recall that Lysippus was an atheist.

After Archias' unexplained disappearance, Lysippus married Archias' wife and lived a long and happy life, writing music. Among other notable achievements, he invented opera. His masterpiece, *Twilight of the Idols*, was a concerted attack on religion and the god delusion. It sparked off a wave of free thinking and made atheist both acceptable and fashionable. There will, of course, be a backlash and all copies of Lysippus' works will be burnt (apart from the ones on my shelves, of course) but the true believers won't be able to turn back the clock. Faith in the gods will gradually die out, and my family— well. I never liked them much, to be honest with you.

My fault, I suppose. Or at least, my doing.

My family always reckoned I was up to something. They were quite right.